About the Author

Sue was born in London, brought up by her grandmother in the south of England and then served as a police officer in Hampshire for many years before retiring and moving to Yorkshire, where she became a shepherd in the Yorkshire Dales. She has sung in operatic societies and choirs all her life. She now lives in the Yorkshire Wolds, writes a weekly diary for a regional paper and cares for two elderly cats.

Going, Going, Gone!

Sue Woodcock

Going, Going, Gone!

Pegasus

Pegasus is an imprint of
Pegasus Elliot MacKenzie Publishers Ltd.
www.pegasuspublishers.com

First Published in 2025

Pegasus
Sheraton House Castle Park
Cambridge CB3 0AX England

Printed & Bound in Great Britain

Dedication

I would like to dedicate this book to Miss Sue Mansergh, my geography teacher at St Swithun's School, who inspired me to love the outside world, and to my friend Tamsin Holding for her care of my dogs.

Acknowledgements

To Rachel Thomson for the cover artwork.

Dramatis Personae.

The Farming Community

James Boothby – father.

Ernest Boothby – grandfather.

Colin Boothby – son.

Robin Goodyard – Farmer neighbour of James Boothby.

John Goodyard, his son.

Cherry Goodyard, his daughter.

Neil Day, wife Lizzie, son Jack, friends of Colin Boothby.

Auction Mart Staff

William Atkins – senior auctioneer (Mr Atkins).

Son William Atkins junior – auctioneer (Mr William).

Son, Edward Atkins – auctioneer (Mr Ted).

Alice Atkins – daughter (deceased).

Harold Potter – auctioneer.

Bridget Whales – office manager.

Cyril Whales – her husband.

Herbert Yorke, wife Sadie, son Bert.

Eddie Oddie – foreman, Norman Ley, Michael Tully, Millie, Doreen (cleaner), Debbie Totton – Margaret – Leyburn Branch. Other associated workers Eric Rees – driver.

Police Officers

PC Des Trotter, local beat officer – wife Aileen.

WPC Chelsea Woods – probationer.

Alf – scenes of crime officer.

Dr Cannon – police surgeon.

Murder Squad

Detective Chief Superintendent Saul Catchpole.

Detective Chief Inspector Alan Withers.

Detective Inspector Geoff Bickerstaff.

Detective Sergeant Tarik Singh.

Detective Sergeant Julie Pellow.

Detective constables Simon, Caroline Withers.

Office Manager Fred Dunlop, Deputy Manager Paddy,
Office Clerk Nita.

The Catchpole Family

Saul – Anna, Jake – Diana, Abraham – Esther.

Sons – Stephen, Sam Sons – Malachi, Ariel,
Isaac (Zach).

Daughters – Sharon, Susan, Daughter – Rachel.

Ruth – Anna's sister.

Animals

Hercules (huge mastiff).

Hector and Lysander – labradors.

Hostel manager – Mrs Clarke.

Philip Pickstaff – railway employee, daughter Alison.

Mrs Uttley – WI member.

George – mortuary attendant.

Chapter 1

James Boothby had enjoyed his day at the auction mart. He had met a number of fellow farmers, had an excellent lunch and all the stock he had brought to the auction had sold very well. He had been found by several purchasers for the luck and had himself been generous. He went to the auctioneer's office to collect his cheque, thinking it would help towards his new lambing shed. Sheep prices were on fire at the moment. He was hoping to stop off at The Bull to celebrate on the way home. He left the office and walked out to the car park towards his Land Rover. His son, Colin, had driven the sheep transporter to the market and should have been home by now. He had last seen him just after lunch. Colin was a good lad; hardworking, strong and committed to farming. They had arranged to meet up at The Bull, which was within walking distance of the farm.

He pulled his keys from his pocket, opened the door of the Land Rover and paused. Their transporter was still in the car park. He walked over to it, hoping to find Colin sleeping in the cab, but it was locked, and the engine was cold. There was no sign of his son. James wondered what to do. He saw a neighbour, Robin Goodyard, heading to his Nissan nearby.

"Robbie, you ain't seen my lad, Colin, have you?"

"I saw him lunch time, not since. Try the pub."

James went to the nearest pub, The Green Man. It was almost empty. He asked but was told that no one had seen Colin all day. Then he tried the Cost Cutter shop next door and the garage nearby, but no one remembered seeing Colin since he had called in there in the morning. He rang Colin's phone but got no reply. He then rang their home and was told by his father that Colin had not returned. Mystified and not a little uneasy, he returned to the transporter and looked for a message there and on his Land Rover. Finding nothing, he went back into the auction mart buildings and checked in the gents and then at the office and all the shops and agricultural merchants in the complex that were still open. The canteen was closing and there was no trace of Colin.

Returning to the transporter, he opened up the back and looked inside. It was empty. He returned to the cattle pens and spoke to the workers there who were hosing the area down. Most of them knew him and Colin. Several of them agreed that they had seen Colin that morning, but no one had seen him after lunch. One old chap, Bert, suggested he look in the bull sales ring, which had only just finished selling. James couldn't find him there either. He wondered where else his lad might be. The offices were being locked up, so he checked the sales rings, starting with the sheep ring. There was nothing there, so he went to the cattle ring. It had not been used that day and was deserted.

On the top tier in the end row of seats, he found fresh blood. In the row below, he found Colin's mobile phone smashed. He hurried down to the office and found the auctioneer, William Atkins, whom he had known for years, and told him what he had found. The auctioneer was the son of the founder of the firm and was a kind man.

He listened and said, "Jim, I don't like the sound of this. I will get a search started. I'll call everyone in on the tannoy and call for your son as well."

The staff soon collected, and a search began. Several times, a call went out for Colin. William Atkins went to the cattle ring and looked at the blood and the phone. He touched nothing; he called the local police officer.

The auction mart was a huge area to search. Each member of staff took a section. PC Trotter arrived with his probationer, WPC Chelsea Woods. They went to the cattle ring and looked at the blood and the phone. They knew something had been found when they heard screams from the stairwell just behind the locked door next to them. Mr Atkins quickly unlocked the door and they found the cleaner, Doreen, at the bottom of the stairwell. Doreen had splendid lungs and an ample frame and once she had started screaming, she couldn't stop.

Mr Atkins and the two police officers went down the stairs. Behind some cardboard boxes was a body. Someone took Doreen away and soon, several people had assembled and James rushed up, pushed his way through and stood staring at the legs that were sticking out from the boxes. PC Trotter had called for assistance and held James back. Carefully, he moved one of the boxes to reveal a pool of congealing blood by the Wellington boots they could see.

James said, "That's not Colin."

"Are you sure?"

"Of course, I am. I do know my own son."

PC Trotter felt for a pulse and could find none. The body was cold. He moved everyone back and Mr Atkins said, "All of you keep searching and tell us if you find anything unusual. We must find young Colin. Bert, please, will you take Doreen to the office and get her a brandy?"

"Yes, Mr William, I will. Er, PC Trotter, I know who that is."

"Who?"

"It is Eric who drives for Oldham's animal transporters. I could have sworn I saw him leave. He had a load of sheep to take to the buyer over in Lancashire. I saw him drive off. I had helped him load the sheep up. About two it was."

"You are sure it was him driving, not just loading for someone else to take away?"

"Yes, he got into the driver's seat. He had the keys and unlocked the door, got in and I handed him the movement order."

"So where is his animal transporter?"

"I'll check the yard now. Mr William, will you ring the firm?"

"Yes, Bert, I will. Was anyone with him in the cab?"

"Not that I saw. There weren't many people around, just a couple of farmers, what I know, oh and young Michael and his mate, Norman, who were loading sheep for Mr Hicks into his trailer."

"Was Colin Boothby around?"

"No, Officer, he wasn't. Not then, I saw him about lunchtime."

"Well, we need to find him. Chelsea, go to the office with Mr Atkins please, and ask to use the phone there. Ring the control room and ask for Scenes of Crime, a police surgeon and the circus; they will understand. Tell them we have a suspicious sudden death. Then, take everyone's details here and find out who was at the auction today. Mr Atkins, when was this area last checked? When was the cattle ring last used?"

"Yesterday for the cattle ring, and Doreen will know about here. I locked the cattle ring as soon as I saw the blood and the phone."

Chelsea had not long been out of training school. She was a city girl from down south and the whole place was rather like an alien planet to her. She did as her tutor constable, PC Trotter, had asked and after ringing the control room, carried out their instructions.

At the desk next to her, as she was making the call, was Bridget, who had worked in the auction office for many years.

Bridget was a motherly and capable woman, and she took pity on Chelsea. "Here, lass, sit down. I've got all those records you will be wanting and I'm printing copies for you. You look a bit lost?"

"I am. I have only just started and I'm not from around here or from farming. I am terrified I will do something wrong!"

"Well, I know you ain't from round here; your accent tells us that. I am sure PC Trotter will look after you. I've known Des Trotter for years; he's a good chap. When he first came here, he didn't know much either. You say everyone's to stop on, so I've got the canteen staff to get the cookers and kettles on. We're asking everyone to wait in the canteen when they have finished searching. I'll get us a cuppa in here; young Lucy is bringing a tray."

"Thanks, Mrs Whale, you're very kind."

"You call me Bridget, dear; I hear you are called Chelsea?"

"That's right."

"I went there once when I was down in the smoke with the Horticultural Society for the Flower Show. There were that many people I never saw much; we had a good evening at a really posh pub."

Chelsea looked at the pile of sales dockets and movement orders in front of her. Bridget kindly handed her two cardboard boxes and helped her sort the papers into two piles.

"Bridget, I know I don't know much, and I don't want to look a twit, but I thought it was sheep and calves that were sold today?"

"It was, dear, what's wrong?"

"Then why does it say here Mules and here Hoggs?"

Bridgette laughed. "No, lass, a mule is a kind of sheep, big. The father is a Blue-Faced Leicester Tup and the mother is probably a Swardle. That's a Swaledale to offcumdens like you; that's a local type of sheep with a black face and legs. Lives up on the moors. A hog is older than a lamb, can be any breed."

"Oh, I see, so what is a tup?"

"You'd know it as a ram. It's just northern talk. You'll soon pick it up. What made you come up north, anyway?"

"My parents have moved abroad to South Africa, and I need to settle somewhere. My brother is at Leeds University, so I thought I might try to be near him."

"Where are you living?"

"I am trying to find somewhere half decent; I am in the YWCA at the moment. I hate it there."

"You want digs? What are you looking for?"

"Somewhere round here, just a room, preferably with a bathroom and a small kitchen, nothing fancy."

"Do you mind animals?"

"What kind of animals?"

"Farm animals."

"I don't know!"

"It's just we've got my mum's old granny flat at the farm. She died last year. It's got a bedroom, small kitchenette, sitting room and bathroom. It's even got a little garden of its own. We were talking about getting a lodger only last night, but you never know who you're getting. Are you interested?"

"I doubt I could afford a lot."

"We'll see. Give me your number and I'll talk it over with my Cyril and ring you."

"You don't even know me!"

"I know what you do, you'll be honest if nothing else, or you wouldn't be a copper. If Des Trotter says you're sound, that will be good enough for us. I'll ask him. Here, I think this call is for you."

Chelsea spoke again with her control room and then went and found Des Trotter, who was stalwartly guarding the stairwell where the body was. She gave him the message and told him what she had done.

He nodded and commented, "Well done! This is a bit like throwing you in at the deep end! I've only ever had a body like this once in all my years in the force. This is not your normal Sudden Death report; we get lots of them. Now I've kept a log, see. I've written down everything and everybody who has come near. Is your pocketbook up to date?"

"Yes, I've recorded everything like you showed me."

"Good girl. Yes, well done. The reason I say is that I expect we will have senior officers all over the place and they will want to check. You being looked after up in the office?"

"You mean tea, coffee?"

"I do. Get this mug back to the canteen, will you, on your way back to the office?"

Chelsea told him about Bridget and her offer. He smiled and said, "I don't know why I didn't think of it before. I dealt with her mother's sudden death last year. You'll not go wrong with them, nice old-fashioned Yorkshire folk. They've no children; couldn't have them. If you take up her offer, she'll mother you, treat you as one of her family and probably expect you to eat with them sometimes, like Sunday lunches. Would you mind?"

"No, I think I might rather like that. I am a dreadful cook."

"Then learn from her. She does the best Yorkshire pudding around, not to mention scones."

"Won't it be awkward; will she not be a suspect? This is a murder enquiry, isn't it?"

"Yes, I see, I'll ask for you. I expect it will be Mr Catchpole that comes out. He's approachable."

"Him? I get to meet him? the chief super? Why is everyone so scared of him?"

"I dunno. He's always been straight with me. I like the man. He doesn't suffer fools, though, but I expect he will talk to you, find out what you know, see you've done it right and if you have, he will say well done. If you haven't, he'll explain where you have gone wrong. He'll only do it once, though."

"Gosh, two weeks in and I get to meet him!"

"Yes. Have they found Colin Boothby yet?"

"No, but they haven't finished searching."

"Then get back to the office. If you are sure, you don't mind being treated as a daughter to Cyril and Bridget, tell her I say you are all right and I will square it with the bosses."

"I don't mind. My mother died when I was little. My stepmother is a bitch. She never did like me much. I left home as soon as I could. My dad was always at work and didn't see what went on. They adore my half-brother and so do I, but I never had much fuss made of me."

"Then be prepared to be smothered! You tell Bridget that and she will probably adopt you there and then. Cyril, he's a kind chap, quiet like most farmers but he is gentle. He told me they needed someone young around. He had a farm lad there, but he was a bad lot. I took the lad to court for burglary and all sorts. They even tried to help him, but he wouldn't accept it. Instead, he pinched from them and the old lady. They were heartbroken about it. Come to think of it, I believe he works here now, on the yards. I rather think that Bridget got him taken on here when he came out of the Young Offenders place. Norman Ley is his name and the is a thoroughly bad lot. Cyril won't have him back there."

"They sound lovely. Do you think they will understand about shift work?"

"Aye, I am sure they will. Here, take this mug and get back. Unless you know anyone is from CID, ask for identification. It's expected and put an entry in your book."

In the canteen, Chelsea was given another tray of cups of tea for the office. The room was full as she left the canteen, with many men talking at the tables as they sat and waited. She noticed many of them staring at her.

Two men got up and politely opened the door for her as she came into the office and put the tray down on the table beside Bridget, who commented, "I see Milly is looking after us. Sit down, lass, and could you pass me that yellow file there? It is a list of all our regular customers, and I expect you will be needing it. I've also made a list of all the hauliers we use. I've put some other bits in your tray that you might need. Is Des Trotter all right down there?"

"Yes, stalwartly guarding the body. He says to tell you my coming to you is all right with him."

"Good. I've just rung Cyril; he says to offer it to you. Would £50 a week be fair, including bills except the telephone? I'll do your washing for that, and you will be welcome to eat with us if you want to. I always cook too much anyway. You will be very welcome, lass. Very welcome indeed."

"I don't think that's enough. I pay £70 now just for a basic room."

"Nay, lass, as Cyril says, the place needs redecorating and the furniture is old-fashioned and shabby. We will need to get it done out before we can charge much. Fifty will do."

"I'll redecorate it if you like. I like doing that kind of thing."

"We will help you. Does you play loud music?"

"No, I'm tone-deaf, anyway. Why?"

"Pity, I like a good tune. It is very quiet in there, double glazed, insulated all that. You will be wanting quiet, sleeping off of nights and that. You had better come and see it soon."

"Thanks, I will. Actually, I can make covers and curtains. I have a good sewing machine and before I joined this job, I worked as an interior designer. I learned a lot."

"Looks like we will get on fine! Here is the address and how to find us; I've put our phone number on there too. Move in as soon as you like if it takes your fancy. I'll try to get it clean for you."

"I can do that. When I am off duty, I don't know anyone yet, so I won't be going out much and it will give me something to do. Can I ask a question?"

"Yes, dear, go on."

"Why did everyone stare at me in the canteen just now? Normally, I get the odd whistle and occasionally a suggestive comment or two. They were all so polite. Why?"

"Oh, I see. Well, with your looks, I can see that might happen, but folk round here are rather reserved, almost too polite sometimes. It will take a while for them to break through their natural reserve. You's a good-looking lass. That's why they were staring. You'll find farming folk keep their counsel until they know you. They meant no harm by it; you will soon be accepted."

"I wondered if they didn't like me."

"They are suspicious of any stranger, especially a rozzer. They knows Des Trotter accepted him a long time back. He is well-liked, fair and does his job well. He has been right good to most folk round here. He was kind when my mum died and before helped with a lad that went wrong."

"Norman, yes, he said tell me where do you think Colin Boothby is?"

"I dunno. It's a right mystery. Nice lad, sound as a pound. I've known him since he was a nipper. He was courting a lass over Hellifield way. Her dad is a driver on the railway. It broke young Colin's heart when she died, most unexpectedly that was. Poor lad, he was gutted. Some sort of virus affected her heart, we were told. She was laid to rest down the road from here, in the churchyard."

"Could he be visiting her grave, do you think?"

"He might, yes. It's not far from here. Shall I get my Cyril to check on the way here? He has to pass there to come and get me."

"Would you, what was her name?"

"Alison Pickstaff. My Cyril knows where 'cos we went to the funeral. The father moved away. I believe he lives up near Carlisle now, a place called Lazonby; he still works for the railway."

As they waited, Chelsea asked, "Do you know this Eric, the driver?"

"On yes, he's a regular here. Quite the ladies' man. He'd chat up anything in a skirt. Even tried it on with me once and was most offended when all I could do was laugh at him. He tried several times to get me to go out to his truck with him, but I wasn't falling for that. Young Debbie, who works here, she did once but came running back in, most upset but wouldn't say why. She won't even look at him now; well, she won't have to now, will she? She's in the canteen now. I wouldn't trust Eric as far as I could throw him. It's not like he was a looker, by the way; he fancied himself no mistake. Did you see has had a cast in one eye?"

"I'm afraid I couldn't see much of his face."

"Oh dear, how horrid, you mean someone bashed his head in?"

"I can't say. I didn't get that close. It was bad enough just being there."

"Why didn't you say? It must have shaken you up. Here, have another cuppa. It'll calm your nerves."

"Thanks. Tell me about Norman."

Chapter 2

By the time the duty inspector arrived, Chelsea had been told almost every worker's life history, who was related to whom, where they lived and who they had been seeing. She had noted it all down. The inspector told her to stay where she was and went down to PC Trotter, and then went and joined in the search for Colin Boothby.

A tall, slim man with slightly greying ginger hair and with a slight limp, wearing a grey suit and carrying a briefcase, walked in.

He looked down from his considerable height, smiled and said, "Hello, I am Chief Superintendent Catchpole. Who are you?"

"WPC Chelsea Woods, sir. May I see some identification?"

"Of course, quite right to ask. Here's my warrant card. Well, done, Officer, logging it into your book. Can you take me to see this body?"

"Certainly, sir, this way."

As they walked along the corridor, Saul Catchpole looked down at Chelsea and saw a stunningly beautiful young officer beside him. "Are you new? I don't remember seeing you before."

"Yes, sir, two weeks out of training school, attached to PC Trotter, sir."

"Des Trotter, yes. He is a good officer; you will learn a lot from him. He is well thought of locally and within the force. I didn't know he was a tutor constable."

"I'm his first sprog, sir. He only agreed to puppy walk me when PC Giles retired."

"I see. You have done well, WPC Woods. I'll come back and talk to you later. I suspect you have found out quite a lot while you have been here. Detective Chief Inspector Withers will be joining me and a Detective Sergeant Singh. Could you bring them down to me when they arrive? Meanwhile, keep talking to the office staff here; I think you might learn a lot from them."

"Yes, sir. Can I bring you a tea or coffee?"

Saul laughed. "You will do well both locally and on the job. You learn fast; I can see that. No, I'll have one when I come and see you."

"Sir, I hope I have done the right thing. I was asking Bridget Whale in the office about the missing lad, Colin Boothby. She told me he'd been courting a girl who died. I wondered if he had gone to visit her grave near here. She offered to ring her husband to go and see. Everyone was busy, so I said yes. He is on his way there now."

"Quick thinking, well done. Yes, you did the right thing. Let me know if the lad turns up, please. Where is the father of the lad?"

"In the office with the auctioneer, Mr Atkins, who everyone refers to as Mr William."

Saul approached PC Trotter and had a quick look at the body and standing up again, said, "Thank you, PC

Trotter. You can be proud of WPC Woods; she has done very well, a credit to both of you."

Chelsea went back to the office. The copious cups of tea had meant that she needed the loo. She hoped to use the staff one near the office, but Doreen was in residence. She asked Bridget where the main toilets were.

"There is the public one near where the body is, so I expect it is blocked off at the moment. There is another; it is seldom used down in the basement. Here, I'll get the keys and show you. The place hasn't been used in a while."

Bridget went to the safe and removed a bunch of keys from it and unlocked a door in the office that Chelsea had assumed was a cupboard. She switched on a light and together they went to the top of a flight of stairs, leading to a long corridor. "Down the corridor, it is the door at the end. The light switch is on the right-hand side."

Chelsea peered down the corridor, noticing several doors on either side. "What do you keep down here?"

"Mainly records, we have a couple of secure storerooms, a strong room and a first aid store and humane killers in case we need them. A few chemicals for cleaning. We have to have things like that in case a bull goes mad, or there is an emergency. It is seldom used."

Chelsea walked down the corridor, passing several doors. She paused at one, which was slightly ajar but then saw the toilet in front of her, unlocked the door and put on the light. There was very dim lighting there. When she had done, she washed her hands at the sink, having put the toilet lid back down. As she was drying her hands on some paper towel, she heard a splat sounding a bit like a drip from the area of the toilet. Wondering if a pipe was leaking, she took a small Maglite torch from her belt and went to look. A second drip hit the toilet lid as she drew near. It splashed her hand, and she froze. In the dim light, it looked like blood. Then, she saw a pool of blood on the floor by the back of the toilet. She looked up as two more drops came down. The ceiling was made of tiles, two of which were moved and beyond them was some green material and a hand. The tiles were heavily stained with blood. She wondered if she was actually under the stairwell but did not think so. She drew back, locked the toilet door and ran back along the corridor and up the stairs into the office.

Bridget looked at her in horror and said, "Whatever is the matter, lass? You're as white as a sheet. Is that blood on you? Have you had an accident?"

"No, but someone has. Don't let anyone down there until I get back."

She ran down to PC Trotter, who was with Mr Catchpole and two other uniform officers.

Mr Catchpole looked at her in surprise and said, "What is wrong, officer?"

"I think you had better come with me, sir. I've found something. I think it is someone dead or seriously injured."

Mr Catchpole said, "PC Trotter, you stay here. You two others come with me. Show me, please."

They hurried down the corridor to the basement, and Chelsea handed her torch to him as she unlocked the door to the toilet. Mr Catchpole went in and looked up and then climbed up on the toilet basin and looked into the ceiling space. The two others followed him while Chelsea watched. She felt cold and found she was shaking. Feeling a little lightheaded, she leaned against the corridor wall. Her teeth were chattering. One of the officers came out and ran back upstairs.

Not long after, Mr Catchpole came out of the toilet. He, too, was splattered in quite a lot of blood. He looked at her and said, "Sit down before you fall down. Yes, it is a body. Well done!"

Chelsea sank to the ground and sat leaning her back on the wall. She uttered, "I'm all right, I'm all right. It was just a bit of a shock."

Saul sat beside her and quietly said, "I expect it was. Here, child, catch your breath. How come you were down here?"

Chelsea explained with some embarrassment. He laughed and said, "Quite natural, don't worry. I understand. It isn't nice. I feel bad even now, after many years. I expect you are a bit shaken up. You did very well, you know. Did you hear or see anything while you were down here?"

"No, sir, I still have the keys. Can I give them to you?"

Together, they stood up and slowly walked back towards the stairs.

Chelsea paused and said, "That's odd. When I came down here, that door there was ajar. I thought it strange but didn't go in. Now it's shut."

"Was it, how far ajar?"

Chelsea showed him. "About this much. Four, five inches maybe."

"You're sure?"

"Certain. I know it was that one; it has the green first aid sign on it."

Saul tried the door, but it was locked. He looked down at the floor and whispered, "You're right. It has recently been opened; look at the large footprint there and the broken cobweb."

"Thanks for believing me."

"I did, anyway."

He quickly found the right key, turned the lock and indicated for her to stand behind him. He opened the door and put his hand inside to find the light switch in the room. There was a loud bang, a smashing noise and a thud and he was thrown backwards with some force out of the room. The door slammed shut and together, he and Chelsea rushed to push it open, but it was firmly blocked by something. They could hear movement from inside the room and the sound of furniture being dragged up to the door.

Saul said, "Get help, quickly."

Chelsea ran as fast as she could up to the office where she found several police officers and told them, and then followed them back down the stairs. Together, several officers managed to force the door in. It gave way with a loud crash and most of the officers went into the room. She was about to follow them in, but Saul waved her back and they stood in the corridor waiting while the officers searched the room. Something, she wasn't sure what, made her look up. There was movement above she could see there was someone above the ceiling tiles by the way they were flexing. She pointed up and Saul looked with her. They followed the movement until it stopped at what looked like a breeze block wall, which was by the door saying Boiler Room. Saul whispered, "Stick with me. We've called the dogs in. Try the door handle; see if it is locked."

It was. He found the key on the key ring and turned the lock. They very carefully opened the door and Chelsea shone her torch inside but there was no one there. She switched the light on, and they had a quick look around. It was obvious that someone had been sleeping in there. They found a pile of dirty clothes on the floor. They looked up and saw a hole in the ceiling. They exited the room and Saul locked the door. A uniformed inspector came down and told them that the building was surrounded, and the dog team were ready to go in, and they should leave and go up to the office.

Saul handed him the keys, explained what they had seen and found, called the other officers out of the first aid room and the toilet and they all went upstairs.

The inspector asked, "Are we certain the chap in the ceiling is dead?"

The officer who had looked with Saul replied, "Yes, sir. Throat cut, almost decapitated."

"Is it Colin Boothby?"

"Doesn't answer the description, no. Much older, heavier, shorter."

"Well, where the hell is he then?"

"Don't know. We have roadblocks on for miles, sir, and the helicopter is up. All we can do is keep looking."

Saul nodded. "Yes, WPC Woods, can you ask if Mr Whale has checked the churchyard?"

In the office, in proper lights, she saw how blood-spattered Saul was. He also seemed to be bleeding from a cut on his hand. Bridget took one look at him, took a first aid kit from the wall and advanced on him.

"Sit down, Mr Senior Policeman and let me look at that. Then, can you explain why this poor child is cold, white, shaking and looks about to throw up? Sit down and do as you are told; I'm a qualified nurse."

Saul Catchpole knew authority when he met it. He meekly sat down and looked up at her. "You must be Mrs Whale. I am sorry, did I frighten you? Someone, look after WPC Woods, please."

Chelsea interrupted, "I'm all right, sir, really, just a bit shaky; how about you?"

"Absolutely furious, no, not with you. You did very well, I didn't. I actually had hold of him for a moment until he hit me with something. I grabbed a piece of his clothing. It is in my pocket; I'll just take it out."

Bridget stood in front of him. "Oh no, you don't! Let another officer remove it. That is a nasty cut. I doubt it will need stitches, just a dressing. Stay still, man; yes, it will sting a bit; it has got a few large splinters in it."

"Hold on, madam, can I take them out?"

"Who might you be?"

"Scenes of Crime. If he has been in contact with a murderer, we need to take any available evidence. I'll take

35

a couple of swabs and from you, lass, if you don't mind, in case that blood on you is not all that of the victim."

Saul, with a sigh, said, "He is quite right; go ahead. Please feel free to operate on me! No doubt you will want my jacket as well?"

"I am afraid so, and your trousers. You too, lass, we will get some goon suits in here."

Bridget decided things had gone far enough. "Well, you are not taking them until I get something warm for the both of them. Milly lass, can you go to our cloakroom, look in the property box, and get some of those clothes that get left? Fleeces and I am sure there are some jogging bottoms. They have all been washed. We keep them for a year, and if they are not claimed, we give them to the Age UK shop. They were due to go last month. Find something that will fit them. I reckon he is a size forty-inch chest, and she is a size twelve. Right, yes, thought so."

Saul grinned at Chelsea and said, "We do have suits, the white ones we can use."

"Yes, I've seen them on the telly. Made of paper and that thin, you will freeze. As soon as you are done, Mr scientist, I'll dress that cut."

The splinters were quite substantial in Saul's hand, and as one was pulled out, he flinched. "Keep still, sir, please."

"Well, that hurt!"

Bridget said, "Don't be a baby man. You're big enough to bear it."

Saul looked at the Scenes of Crime man, whom he had known for some years, who had a broad grin on his face.

"It's not that funny, Alf!"

"No, sir. Not at all, sir. Now, this is the last one and it will hurt a bit. Brace yourself."

Once the splinters were out, Bridget got to work. Saul was relieved of his suit jacket; his personal things were taken out and put on the desk. He indicated a piece of grey material with a button in it as the item was torn from his assailant. It was bagged up as evidence. Milly came in with an armful of clothes while Bridget dressed the wound and cleaned his hand.

She turned, rummaged through the pile and presented him with a sky-blue fleece top and a pair of jogging bottoms. "These should do for you; I think they are your size."

"Must I have the sky blue one? Can't I have that dark blue one?"

"No, it's too small. What is wrong with the sky-blue one? It matches your eyes."

A smothered laugh came from Alf. Saul gave in. He took his new clothes and disappeared into the staff toilet and changed.

Chelsea had the choice of a dark green top or a pink one. She chose the dark green one, put it on and began to feel a little warmer. Several more CID officers arrived. Saul briefed them and then said, "WPC Woods, Chelsea, isn't it? Please go with Sergeant Pellow here and she will get a statement from you. I know you could do your own, but I need this right the first time. Are you still cold?"

"No, sir, I am fine now."

"Well, I'm not. Mrs Whale, thank you, and please could I buy some hot drinks?"

"No, you can't. They are already on the way, together with some sandwiches. Mr William said you were to be looked after. Now, can I show someone all these lists I've been making for you? Shall we go to the restroom? It is getting a bit busy in here. Mr William is opening the bar if anyone wants more than a tea, coffee or chocolate."

Chapter 3

In the office of Mr Willian Atkins, the auctioneer, James Boothby was talking to DCI Alan Withers, who had calmed him down and told him everything that was being done to find Colin. Mr William was also there, at James' request.

Detective Sergeant Tarik Singh knocked the door, came in and called Alan out. He updated him. Alan asked, "Is Saul all right, not badly hurt?"

"No, not according to the nurse. I thought I should warn you; Saul is bright red in the face."

"That means he's furious about something. I can guess with himself."

"So he says. The dogs have picked up a track from a sewage pipe at the back of the building. Leading out to the main drain by the railway bridge. They have tracked it to a lay by, where it stops. There, we found some recent tyre marks, but it doesn't help much."

"Let me guess, probably a Land Rover?"

"Yes, why do you think that?"

"Doesn't every farmer have one round here?"

"One of the lads suggested it was a Mark Two Land Rover and noticed it was dripping oil. Have you finished with Mr Boothby? If you have, I'll get someone to go home with him. Simon is already there with the grandfather. I've rung his mother. She has married again and living in Wales. She knows nothing."

"What is this about his girlfriend's grave?"

"Someone's been there very recently. Flowers are on the grave bought this morning at the local garage down the road. Two sets of footprints, one bunch of flowers, some of which were scattered about. I've got it all: recorded photos and the like. The garage cannot remember selling them. They were paid for with cash. Oh, and the police surgeon has been, reckons the time of death for Eric Rees was between two and three, and the other chap not long after."

"Tarik, is anyone missing from the staff here?"

"Three. One is Norman Ley, who is a local villain; he went to the gents while they were searching for Boothby and never reappeared; his mate, Michael Tully, went to look for Norman and never came back and the other is an older chap, Herbert Yorke. He was last seen in the canteen just before PC Trotter arrived. His car is in the car park and his boots in his locker; his smart ones that he changes into after he finishes work here. He answers the description of the second body."

"See if anyone can identify him; try Bert; he seems to know everyone."

"Will do. I'll ask Trotter; he might know. That young probationer, she's done very well."

"Yes, she looks bright. Stop drooling over her, you pervert!"

"I'm not the only one."

"I'd noticed."

Alan went back into the office. James Boothby looked at him and then down at the floor.

"You think because my lads disappeared and there have been two dead bodies found that he has killed them and then run away, don't you?"

"Not necessarily, no. It is a possibility, of course, but not the only one, which is why we are trying to find him. He may himself be in danger."

"At least you are honest about it. I'll tell you, he's soft. Can't even kill a lamb. I have to if the need arises. We had a heifer die, slipped in the yard and broke its back. He was fond of it and cried like a baby. He is a gentle lad. He was really cut up when his girlfriend died."

"So, I understand. Did he often visit her grave?"

"I didn't know he had, he never said. Has he been there today?"

"We think so, someone has."

"If it were him, he'd have put roses on it. White ones said she was a splendid Yorkshire lass."

"I'll check."

When all the statements had been taken and everyone had been allowed home, the staff started to close up; William Atkins came to find Saul, who saw them and said,

"Mr Atkins, I can't thank you enough for all the help you and your staff have given us. I am afraid we will have to be here while yet."

"I know, I've spoken with Mr Withers. He said the same. There is an auction here next Tuesday. Do you think it could go ahead?"

"I am sure that will be all right, yes."

"Thank you. I think I need to tell you something. You were searching the pipes under the mart, were you not?"

" Yes, indeed we were."

"Then this may be both relevant and important."

They sat down together in a quiet corner and Saul took his notebook out.

Mr Atkins began, "It isn't about today. It happened a long time ago. My father, Bill Atkins, took over this firm from his dad, my grandfather, also William. I was about twelve then. My brother was seven. We had a sister, Alice, who was nine at the time. In the holidays, we used to play here when there wasn't a sale, sometimes when there was. I know this place like the back of my hand. My brother and sister did, too. I was away, scout camp, I think, when they both went missing one afternoon. I was never told the whole story, but there was a huge search. Somehow, the two of them had found the big drainpipe, crawled up it and taken a wrong turn, not into the basement, which you found via a ventilation shaft, but into the saw tank, where the effluent runs to. They had fallen in and couldn't get out. My brother, Edward, did his best. They hung on and their cries were heard but Alice had gone under several times. She was still alive when they got them both out, but she died in hospital the next day. There was an inquest, of course. Poor Ted, he was so unhappy. The verdict was misadventure, and my dad had the pipe into the saw tank sealed with a grill, and everything was made safe. We never went down there again."

"Yet the access is still there through the basement?"

"That was sealed at both ends with a grill. It still was three months ago. I get it checked; you see. Anyway, my reason for telling you this is that I was clearing out my father's desk when he moved into a smaller office as he is semi-retired now. I found the old newspaper report on it. He had kept it all these years. I asked him if he wanted to keep it. He said he didn't think so, so I left it in his tray in case he did. It disappeared, so I assumed he had either taken it or chucked it."

"Did it describe the pipe and the access?"

"Yes, but not in detail. The coroner recommended it was secured. I rang Dad just now. He says he never found it in his tray assumed I had thrown it out. Someone else must have taken it."

"Oh. Have you been missing anything recently?"

"Funnily enough, yes, we have. Nothing vital, all monies are put in the safe and the officers are locked and alarmed at night. Silly things have been going. A charity box from the canteen that could have been taken by anyone. We reported it to Des Trotter. Some food went missing from the canteen and a box of disposable gloves from the store by the gent's toilets. A box of toilet rolls, some waterproof leggings and one of the agricultural merchants left a bit of his display out, mainly tools, a crowbar, pinch pole, scythe and a few tools. That was on the Saturday. On Monday, the crowbar, the pinch pole and a pair of pliers were gone, and a pair of foot shears and a whole box of foot knives. There was no sign of a break-in."

"Did you report it to us?"

"No, because we sort of knew it had to be an inside job."

"Why?"

"The entrances to the corridors are alarmed and so are the shop doorways; Archie, the agricultural merchant, thought the same. We assumed, therefore, that someone had found a way in. Did your chaps find the grills cut through?"

"All but one, why?"

"The other thing missing was an angle grinder. We kept it in the store if anyone had access in case, we needed to cut any of the gates or take a rough edge off. I have replaced it and now everything like that is in a secure room in the basement."

"You mean the boiler room."

"Yes, in a metal cage in there. The keys are kept in the safe at night and in the main office during the day."

"It is no longer secure. There is an access through the ceiling."

"There shouldn't be; we had the whole room caged in three months ago. Can I go and check?"

"Of course, we will go together. Do you have a suspect?"

"But no direct evidence, yes, of course I do. Norman Ley and his mate Michael Tully. I did ask everyone if they knew anything, I couldn't directly accuse them. They denied knowing anything, but I saw them sniggering just after I asked them."

In the boiler room, the Scenes of Crime officers were just leaving. William Atkins looked and then remarked,

"Yes. The grill has been cut through and quite a bit removed. The cage we built has one side missing. I don't recognise those boxes. Have you looked in them?"

"Yes, sir, we have. We believe they hold the proceeds of some recent burglaries. They were hidden behind the boiler under a fire blanket, which is why they were not spotted, I suspect."

Saul looked in the boxes. "Thanks, Alf. Mr Atkins, have you any idea where they are from?"

"I have never seen them before. What are all these clothes?"

"They were in a pile over there."

"I recognise that jacket there. I've seen Norman wearing it. He said it had been splashed with dairy hypochlorite, our disinfectant, and bleached and ruined and asked for a replacement. I issued him with one and told him to wear what was provided, not personal stuff. When he showed it to me, it had huge white marks on it. Now, it does not. Cunning little bugger!"

"We have an address for him. I think we need to pick him up."

"You may have an address, but he won't be there, so I can tell you that. His aunt chucked him out about three months ago when she caught him nicking again. I'll bet he has been living here since. He always seems to be the first in when he does bother turning up at all. Young Michael, he's just a bit thick; he follows Norman like a puppy. I do know he is still living with his parents. Mind you; I doubt Michael could get through the pipes; he's too fat and too big-boned. Norman is built like a whippet and very strong."

"Why did you take him on, knowing his background?"

"Several reasons. I was asked to by Bridget, who wanted to help him, and Adrian Fielding, his probation officer, who happens to be in the Rotary with me. He is not the only one here with a past, and we try to believe that people can turn over a new leaf. When he does work, Norman is quite handy, especially with livestock, cattle mainly."

"Who else knows about the drain?"

"My brother, he runs our Leyburn branch, but he says he would never go down there again. I won't either. We loved our sister. I couldn't, anyway. Years of good lunches have made me too fat! You might just fit, but it would be a tight squeeze."

"No, thanks! I spoke to the dog handler, who did go down. He is built like a racing snake, and he didn't enjoy it much. Did you ever find the original angle grinder?"

"No, it was a good one, too, a Bosche."

Alf looked up and said, "I think it was found by the grill that is still intact. Sir, I know they found one."

"Thanks, Alf. Mr Atkins, we will bring it to you to see if you can identify it. I do need to know who keeps keys to everywhere, and the alarms?"

"I do. Our office manager, Bridget Whale, who I would trust with my life, my father and our foreman, Eddie Oddie, oh and my son, have a set as well. He is qualifying at the moment, and my brother has a set too,"

"How long has Herbert Yorke worked here?"

"Years. He's a lovely chap. His father worked for mine, and his son has applied and has been here for work experience. Herbert and I almost grew up together; why?"

"I am sorry, but we have reason to believe the other body is Herbert Yorke."

"Oh no, no, no! Not Herbert, please, no. Are you sure?"

"Reasonably, we need an official identification."

"Then I will do it. If you need me to, I would rather than put Sadie, his wife, through that. Oh, God, no. Herbert is, was, the most faithful chap, utterly straight, and my friend from boyhood. Not brilliant but solid, reliable, trustworthy. I hope it isn't, but I need to know. If it is, I will go and see Sadie and break it to her and young Brian. I am Brian's godfather."

"Would you be willing to do it now? We have him upstairs waiting to be moved to the mortuary."

William Atkins almost broke down when he saw the body. "Yes. That is Herbert Yorke, dear God. What caused him to be killed? I was talking to him only this morning."

"What about?"

"I asked him to count the trestle tables in the store and the table clothes, as we are hosting an antiques fair next month. The storeroom is underground too, but not locked. The stairs lead down from where you found that chap."

"Could there be a way through the ceiling from that area to the basement?"

"I suppose so. It is only blocked with breeze blocks. Certainly, if you are down in there, you can hear the toilet flush."

"So, he might have heard something?"

"He might well have, and I sent him down there! Can I go? I'd best tell Sadie. She will be worried as he should have been home by now."

"Certainly. One of my officers will go with you if you don't mind."

"I think I will pick my wife up on the way. She can help. She and Sadie have been friends for years."

Saul went and found Des Trotter and Chelsea Woods. They were in the bar area writing up their pocketbooks.

A middle-aged man came up to Saul and said, "I'm Eddie Oddie. I heard about Herbert. We are all rather cut up about it. It's a real shock; he was a grand chap. Would you mind if I opened the bar and gave anyone who wants it a drink?"

"Not at all. You must all be shaken up."

"I meant your lot, too; they told me to ask you as you are in charge."

"That is kind, but we cannot accept a gift, but I will happily buy one if we need it."

"I'll make tab up for you."

Soon, the bar area was full, but the mood was subdued. Saul sat down beside Chelsea. "How are you feeling now? Better?"

"Yes, sir, thanks. It helps to have something to do. I have already admitted it to Des. I was sick, but since then, I have eaten a sandwich and feel okay now."

"Quite understandable. Dealing with violent death takes some getting used to. Des, before Chelsea, here found the second body. There was something you wanted to ask me. What was it?"

"Oh yes, thanks for remembering. It is concerning Chelsea here. She has been offered good digs at Cyril and Bridget Whale's place; a granny flat. We wondered if you would have any objections, seeing as how the murders have happened here."

"You mean, do I suspect the lady? No, I do not. Chelsea, so long as you don't mind being mothered and if you are happy, by all means, go ahead."

"Thank you. She said as soon as I like. I am in a hostel at the moment and hate it."

"If it is where I think it is, I understand. Miles to travel to work, and noisy and in a very bad area. No, by all means, take up the offer. I need to thank both of you for what you have done today. You have done exactly what was needed and made life easier for me, especially you, Chelsea. You kept your head acted sensibly and courageously. You are also very observant and quick-thinking."

"Thanks, sir, I did my best."

"Des, I have spoken to your divisional commander; I want to borrow you and Chelsea for a while to work with the squad. Do you mind?"

"No, not at all, sir. I can help. I know almost everyone around here. Be pleased to."

"Then can you be here by nine in the morning in Civi's? Both of you?"

On the way out of the car park, Saul met Alan Withers. Saul said, "What are you grinning at?"

"Nothing Saul. You just look so fetching in that sky-blue top that matches your baby-blue eyes!"

"Watch it, Mowgli! I just knew that would get round, you cheeky cub. It is actually very warm and comfortable. Are you heading back to the office?"

"No, Geoff's taken over there and says there isn't a lot we can do tonight, so to go home."

"Then that is what we should do, oh and Trotter and Woods will be joining us tomorrow."

"Now, there is a surprise. They both did very well today. It was inevitable. You usually grab someone local. No sign of young Boothby yet?"

"No, that worries me. I have a bad feeling about it. Is there an all-ports warning out on him?"

"Yes, hours ago. His father says he doesn't even have a passport. I got the river checked from here to past the churchyard, no trace."

"Right, ring me at home if anything comes up."

Chapter 4

Chelsea went to see the hostel manager when she got in.

"Hello, Mrs Clarke. How much notice do you need? I have found some digs closer to where I am working."

"Actually, none. We're fully booked with a waiting list. If you want to go tomorrow, I'll not charge you for this week. Not that we want you to go Chelsea, but I know you would rather have somewhere of your own and it is noisy here. You're a bit older than most of the girls, more grown up. I do understand but you can come back if you need to."

"Thanks. I'm almost packed anyway. I'll leave my keys in the morning."

"Right, dear, I'll get you your deposit. Can I just check your room?"

"Sure. You know I wouldn't take anything."

"Yes, I have to check; it's the rules."

On Chelsea's door were the usual notes and graffiti with 'pig' and 'oink oink' and other childish comments. Mrs Clarke looked at them and said, "Has this happened before?"

"Every night when I come in. I just tear them up and ignore it."

"Do you know who it is?"

"Yes, but I don't really care. They are young and foolish, and it amuses them. Let the children play."

"I don't think so. Have they done any damage?"

"I have made it good. Cleaned up a bit of mess. Usually, it is make-up. Once, it was bacon fat, which took ages to clear up. It didn't seem worth reporting; it would only have made me more unpopular. I will, however, put in a report to my welfare suggesting other officers are not sent here. It is not fair on them."

"My dear, I am so very sorry. I wish you had said. I could have got it stopped."

"You still can. I am not telling anyone I am leaving. I expect it will be back there tomorrow. Try watching the corridor videos about seven in the evening. That is when it happens, after the warden changes, and usually before I get in. If I am here, I just wait and clear it up after they have gone back to their rooms."

"No wonder you want to leave! I shall get you a refund. You shouldn't have to pay for this."

"Don't bother, but thanks anyway. I doubt there will be any letters for me, but please forward them to the police station if there are. My mobile number will still be the same."

By six the next morning, Chelsea was packed and loaded. After she had handed in her keys, she left the hostel and drove out to the Whales farm, which was called Carnslate Farm. As she drove into the main yard, she was relieved to see there was someone already up and a middle-aged man walking across the yard. He looked up, peered myopically at her and approached the car. "Would you be Miss Chelsea Woods?"

"Yes, and I think you are Mr Whale. I am sorry I am so early, but could I look at the room if it is convenient?"

Cyril peered into her car and said, "And if you don't like the place, what'll you do? Looks like you're on the move already."

"Yes. I am sorry. I couldn't stay in the hostel one more moment. If you have changed your mind, I will find a B and B."

"Nay lass, we've not changed our mind. You're welcome, child; come on in. The tea's mashed. Have a look at the place. No obligation, mind." They went into a warm and cosy kitchen. Bridget gave a cry of delight and reached for another mug from the hook under a shelf.

"Eh, lass, you are welcome. I am so glad you came. While kettles on the hob are boiling, come and see the place. I got it a bit tidy last night."

Chelsea went into her new home and wondered what Bridget's idea of tidying was. The place was immaculate. It was a little old-fashioned in the furniture and décor, but it was clean and not as small as she had expected.

She looked all around. "It's wonderful. I couldn't ask for anything better. Here, I called at the cashpoint on my way. It's a month's rent and I expect you will be wanting a deposit, so I've got that too."

She handed a full envelope to Bridget, who looked into it and said, "Bless you, child. There was no need, but yes, please take it. Cyril, you go and fetch young Chelsea's bags in from the car. Tell me, child, do you have bed linen, towels and all that?"

"I've towels; yes, I was going to buy some bed linen today."

"Don't bother. My mum's stuff was in the airing cupboard. She has no further use for it, so it would only have been chucked. Please use it until you can get what you like. The bed is almost new. It's all right; she passed away in her armchair, which we have in our snug."

The car was quickly unloaded, and Bridget looked at the bags and the sewing machine that Cyril brought in. "Is that all?"

"Yes, all my worldly possessions. It isn't much, is it?"

"You must have other stuff. Stored at home?"

"I don't have one. No, my stepmum threw it all out when they sold up and went abroad. I did manage to save my teddy bear. Only because my brother rescued it for me. I've had to start again. Gradually, I'll get what I want, bit by bit."

They went back into the farmhouse kitchen and Bridget placed a large, cooked breakfast in front of her and a huge mug of coffee.

"Eat it. You'll probably have a long day. We have three sets of keys to the annexe; here they are. If you want me to do your washing, put it in the laundry basket and leave me a set of keys so I can get it."

Chelsea asked Bridget to keep two of the sets of keys and, having established that she could keep her car in one of the barns, enjoyed her breakfast. She privately admitted to herself that she had not had such a delicious meal for some time.

She thanked Bridget, who then said, "Now, don't you be buying eggs or milk because we always have spare. I put some in your fridge, along with a bit of butter and some home-cured bacon."

"That is very kind of you, thanks. Look, I don't want to be rude, but I've got to be at the auction mart by nine, so I must get on."

"I have to be there as well. Cyril normally drops me off."

"Then come with me? I'll take you."

"Bless you, child; it will save Cyril the trip."

Saul had called at his office early and then drove out to the auction mart. There had been no progress in the search for Colin Boothby overnight. As he parked his car in the car park, he saw Chelsea pull up in the space beside him, and he watched Bridget and Chelsea get out. They all walked towards the main buildings.

"You're early, WPC Woods, keen to get to work?"

"Very, sir, I ought to tell you, I have taken up Mrs Whales' offer of lodgings."

"I hope it will be a happy arrangement for both of you. I remember when I joined the job, I was in the residential block and hated it. I found lovely digs with a family as soon as I could. The man was a cobbler, a very good one. His son took over the business, and I still get my shoes from them. I have kept in touch with them all these years.

Good morning, Mrs Whale. May I thank you for all the help you have given us?"

"No problem. How is your hand this morning?"

"The bruising has started to come out, and it is healing, thanks to you."

"Well, let me dress it again later. I've been thinking about young Colin. I've known him since he was a nipper, and I remember. When his mother left, he went through a bit of a bad spell and ran away once, but not to her like we all thought. He was gone three days; he would have been about thirteen then. He walked back into the house like nothing had ever happened. He would never say where he had been, but I found out later he's gone walking and stopped in a shepherd's hut up on the hills. I wondered if he'd done it again."

"Do you know where?"

"Sort of. He'd been over Pen-y-Ghent and over to Littondale. There is only one place there he could have stopped, on Neil Day's farm, right up on Cougar Scar. He and Jack Day were chums. Do you want me to ring the Days and see if they can find him?"

"Would you? I would be most grateful."

"Yes. I know Lizzy Day, we're in the WI together. I'll ask her as soon as I get into the office."

"Thank you. How well do you know Colin?"

"Not that well. But you want to know if I think he killed those two and ran away. I very much doubt it. He is a gentle, sensitive lad. He might run away, but I don't think he would harm anyone."

"What might have caused him to run away, do you think?"

"I do know he was dreadfully upset over that lass when she died. I looked at last year's diary and it is a year this week since they buried her."

"He was still grieving for her?"

"I think he always will. I knew him and the girl's father did not get on. The dad didn't want her to marry anyone. He didn't want her going out at all."

"Do you know why?"

"Only talk but the rumour was that the lass kept house for the father, and he wouldn't even let her get out or get a job. He wasn't well-liked, had a foul temper, I believe and very controlling."

"I will follow that up, thanks."

"If ought else occurs to me, shall I tell young Chelsea here? Now I'll get a coffee organised and I'll tell the canteen to get some butties organised for your lads."

Saul found the duty sergeant and had a long chat with him while the other officers who were arriving were given their specific tasks and sent out to follow up a number of enquiries, including a house-to-house survey of the village and the surrounding area. The auction mart was between the nearest village and the edge of town. Saul had been given the office usually used by Mr Atkins Senior to use. Bridget kept all the officers who were coming and going and those at the Mart well supplied with teas and coffees, and just before lunchtime, she came and found Saul.

"Mr Catchpole, I rang Lizzie Day. Jack and Neil Day, their son, went out and looked for Colin. They have found him, but he is in a state. He's alive but they think he has been injured. They can't get a word out of him. He is shaking and very cold and they say he seems in a sort of daze. They have taken him back to their farm to get him warmed up a bit, then they are bringing him back to his home. They will be there in about an hour."

"Thank God! I was really worried about him. We will have to see him, of course."

"They realise that but say he has obviously been knocked about a bit, so needs to see a doctor. Here is their number; they are expecting your call."

Saul spoke at length to Lizzie Day and then, with his inspector, Geoff Bickerstaff, drove up to the Boothby's farm. Colin had not yet arrived, and they were met by James Boothby and his father, Ernest Boothby.

James Boothby said, "Neil Day rang me just before your control room did. Told me that have found him. Now you'll be wanting to arrest him, I expect."

"Not necessarily, but we will need to talk to him when he is better. I have called our police surgeon who lives locally to come and check him over for you. I am just so glad he is alive."

"We both know he must be your prime suspect."

"He may be a suspect, yes, but until we know what has happened, I try to keep an open mind."

"I hope so; he is not the killing type."

"So, I have been told. Until he can tell us what happened to him, we will not know. It is equally possible that he might have been a victim, you know."

"Did you find out if he went to the grave of that poor girl?"

"Yes, I followed that up. There were white roses on the grave, fresh ones. But we also found some of them strewn around and broken. There were two sets of footprints. Would he have gone to the grave with anyone else?"

"No. The only other person who might have reason to go is that aresehole of a father or hers. Nasty man. He came and saw us when he found out Colin was courting her. He told us to keep young Colin away from her and said he wouldn't have her associating with the likes of us and we were not good enough to even talk to her. I do know he had frightened off several previous boyfriends. Colin is made of sterner stuff. He told me at the time that she was terrified of her father. I liked the lass, and I said if they did want to get together, they could come and live here, and not long after that, we heard she had died. Colin never got to see her again. We went to the funeral; of course, we found out from the vicar when it was. Phil Pickstaff, her father, just glowered at us. There was no wake, nothing. The only flowers on her coffin were the ones Colin had arranged. The only thing Pickstaff said to Colin was that now he could not get his filthy hands on her. Colin was that devastated, he went all quiet and unhappy for months. I thought he was over it, but obviously, I was way off the mark."

"I understand the father moved away."

"Yes, that was odd too. He never spoke to the likes of us again but told someone on the railway that because she died so suddenly like, his neighbours were spreading rumours that her death wasn't natural, and he wasn't going to put up with their insinuations no more."

"Who was the doctor who certified death?"

"That was odd too. Most of us round here go to the local doctor, Dr Cannon, who I think is your police surgeon. He never had anything to do with her. The father called in a doctor from miles away, I don't know who."

"Was her death investigated as a sudden death?"

"No. According to the father, she had been ill for a week or so and it was a virus or something; the funeral was two days afterwards. Coilin only knew because he called to see her, and the father said she had died. Colin rang around and found the undertaker and quite a few turned up. I got the impression that Pickstaff was not best pleased. The undertaker told Colin that the father had wanted her cremated but changed his mind when he was told it would need two doctors to sign off on that."

"I think you are trying to tell me you think her death was not natural and something untoward was going on."

"Yes. I would like her death investigated, and so would Colin. He was so devastated at the time and said that whatever we did, it wouldn't bring her back. He was very upset when the father posted back the ring he had given her. No note, just in a cheap envelope."

"So, you believe that the so-called illness wasn't real?"

"I have no evidence to prove that."

"So why leave it till now to speak out?"

"Colin was so distressed he asked me to leave it."

60

"Then I will investigate. It looks like that might be them now. Is a car coming?"

"No, that is Dr Cannon's car. The Days have a Discovery."

They all went into the farmhouse to await the arrival of the Days. Ernest Boothby went to the kitchen to put the kettle on, and Saul went with him.

Ernest looked up at him and said, "Are you the one in charge?"

"Yes."

"Then I will tell you, don't assume the lad is guilty. You've your job to do but he is no killer. He's a really sensitive lad. He's not been right since the lass died."

"So, I have been told. Do you think she died of natural causes?"

"I had no reason not to at the time, but now I wonder. She went out with another lad before Colin. He and she split up, but he was sweet on her, too. Young Richard Goodyard on the next farm over. That is a strange family and all. I know Colin and Dick had a spat over her long time ago."

It was not long before the Days arrived with Colin. Saul saw a sturdy, young man, with wide set eyes, sandy hair, and a tanned face, which was heavily bruised and was cut in several places. There was also a large cut above one ear which had bled down his jacket. He was limping and looked concussed. He looked around him as if he did not know where he was. Dr Cannon sat him down and said,

"Colin lad, it's Dr Canon. Can you tell me what happened?"

Colin stared at him without any recognition. His face was blank. The doctor turned to Saul,

"He's not right, please call an ambulance asap. I want him in the hospital."

As they waited for the ambulance, Saul said to Ernest, "Can you get some fresh clothes for him and nightwear? We will need his ones."

Shortly afterwards, Ernest came down with a holdall and Inspector Bickerstaff went with Colin and James Boothby to the hospital. The Days came in and Saul asked, "Where did you find him?"

"Up by Cougar Cave, sitting like that, just in the entrance, cold and very bloody. Him and Jack used to play up there as kids. He said nothing but walked with us and we put him on the quad and got him back to the farmhouse. We warmed him up and brought him straight here. It was quicker than if an ambulance had to come to us. He has said nothing. I'm not even sure he knows who we are."

"When did you last see him?"

"A couple of months back. Him and Jack went off on some Young Farmers do."

"How could he have got to where you found him?"

"Well, I do know he walked to the cave over the marsh from the road. There is a right, reedy, boggy bit with recent tracks in it. We found his cap in that, covered in blood. We brought it with us. Are you dealing with these abandoned sheep, too?"

"What abandoned sheep?"

"A hundred and sixteen of them, dumped on the road not far from the cave. Lambs, all of them. The road was unfenced there, and they went all over the place. My neighbour rounded them up with me and his dogs and put them in my barn. We are getting their ear tag numbers checked now. Fit, they looked clean as if just going to market."

"How many would fit in a sheep transporter?"

"About one hundred twenty, why?"

"Because we are missing a load from the auction mart yesterday. Did they all have the same numbers?"

"No, several different ones."

They very quickly established that the sheep were those that had been loaded onto the missing trailer at the market. Saul rang Mr William Atkins and confirmed they were the sheep from the missing trailer. Saul said to Mr Day, "Did Colin have any signs of being close to sheep?"

"Well, his coat was covered in sheep muck; looked like he'd been lying in it. I saved the coat; it is with the cap."

"Do you know if anyone saw the transporter in your area?"

"I'll ask. That road comes past our farm. We did hear a big vehicle late last night. Our road is not really suitable for big lorries. We heard one reversing to take the corner near the bridge and then we heard it struggling, in what sounded like the wrong gear going up the hill but by the time I got to the window, all I could see was the lights going up the road. Made a right mess of the grass on the corner. It was about eleven, just as I was heading to bed. I was in the bathroom when I heard it and had to go to the front of the house to see."

"Do you think it was laden?"

"No. If it had a load on, it would have gripped better on the mud and grass. I looked this morning; it made a right mess and even knocked a bit of the bridge wall down."

"I think I had better have a look. Where would it have gone from there?"

"That's the point. It would have come out at the Malham turn, but it is tricky with a vehicle that size. Someone must have seen or heard it. I was going to ring the farmer up the road last night, but it was late, and something distracted me."

"May I ask what?"

"I'd put my coat on and boots and was going to check the wall by the corner. Something had excited the dogs in the yard. They went out of the kitchen through the dog flap, and what interested me was they were excited but not barking. They bark at any stranger. They were alert but were watching something down by the stream. I went out, saw the wall was down, and then the dog settled down and I came back in. I mended the wall first thing this morning before Bridget rang us."

"Could it have been a fox or something like that?"

"No way. They bark like crazy at a fox, a badger, or a deer. They even bark at rabbits. It was most strange."

"As if they knew whoever it was, a friend?"

"You mean young Colin. Why didn't he come to us instead of up to the cave? He knows he's always welcome. We would have helped him?"

"Would they have barked at him?"

"No, you're right. They know and like him. Why did he not come to me? I was out there a while?"

"We will have to ask him when he's better. Maybe he was scared."

"He's no reason to be scared of us; how did you work it out about the dogs?"

"I read my Conan Doyle. Sherlock Holmes made a case of a dog not barking during the night."

"If you say so, I prefer westerns myself. The way that vehicle was being driven, I wouldn't be surprised if it went off the road. I'll ring some of the farmers up there and ask them if they know 'owt. What do we do with these lambs?"

"I will ring the auction mart and they can arrange to get someone to pick them up."

By teatime, every farmer in the area had been alerted and was looking for the sheep transporter. A team of police officers had found tracks and paint samples on walls in several places. Saul had gone back to the mart and shortly after, he received a call from a farmer,

"We have found your missing sheep transporter. Someone had driven it through a set of gates into a clearing in a wood; they must have been tanking it. I'll wait for your chaps by the Langcliffe Institute and show them from there. They will never find it on their own."

Saul passed the message on.

Chapter 5

Colin Boothby was not only severely concussed; he was in deep shock and suffering from a severe beating. He was admitted to hospital and when X-rayed, it was discovered he had a fractured skull, which required and immediate operation. His clothes were taken by Inspector Bickerstaff, and his father was happy for swabs to be taken from him.

Inspector Bickerstaff spoke to the doctors and was told it would be some time before he was fit to be interviewed.

"Any idea what caused the fracture?"

"A cylindrical blunt instrument, quite heavy, I should think. Look here on the X-rays. I will get you a copy. Had he not had a very thick bone structure, it could easily have killed him. I will get an exact measurement, but I would suggest some sort of piping?"

"Could it have been a fall from a vehicle or an accident?"

"No way. I think he was hit from behind on the side of the head. You can see it on the X-rays. I'll get you a copy. You can see the depression there; it looks like some sort of piping."

"Is that what is causing him not to speak?"

"I doubt it. I think he is severely traumatised. Is he under arrest?"

"No. I need someone with him in case he says anything. It looks, as you say, that he is a victim. And he is, at the moment, the only person who can tell us what happened."

"He is still very poorly but I think he is out of danger. He won't be going anywhere for a while; we can tell you if he does say anything."

"It isn't just that. If someone tried to kill him, they might well want to finish the job. We need to protect him."

"Oh yes, I see. Do you want him in private room, then?"

"No. I think it might be better if he can be seen easily."

"Yes, I will tell the nursing staff. I will keep you posted as to his progress. I have already given your forensic chap the things we dug out of the wounds. There were some pieces of metal and, some rust flakes and some splinters of wood. It looks like he was taken by surprise. There are no marks on his hands, no defensive marks, you know, bruised knuckles or the like."

When everyone got back to the office, Saul updated the squad. "Having established what we now know, we need to take the next step. I have arranged for the exhumation of Alison Pickstaff's body. The coroner has agreed mainly because the doctor who signed her death certificate has already come under suspicion for several other things. The General Medical Council has, in fact, suspended him pending some other investigations.

The exhumation will be done first thing tomorrow morning. Forensics have found a lot on, or more correctly in, the transporter and we are awaiting the results. Well done, Chelsea, for the contact you have made that sent us to the grave and therefore finding Coilin Boothby. The farming community have been most helpful."

Des Trotter said, "Yes, they are a close-knit community, and my wife has taken any number of calls both offering information and any help we need. I will have to follow all of them up."

"Thank you, PC Trotter, you and WPC Woods."

"We have discovered that Eric, the driver, was quite a nasty piece of work. He has been investigated but never convicted of several counts of indecent assault. Julia is currently interviewing a girl called Debbie at the auction mart, who has stated he tried to rape her once, not long ago. May I suggest that Herbert Yorke overheard or came across something and was an innocent victim?"

"Yes, Tarik, it is possible. Have we picked up Norman Ley yet?"

"No, but we have interviewed his friend Michael. He says he does not know where he is now but admits he knew he was living at the auction mart in the basement. Ley now drives a beaten-up old Land Rover Series 2. I have circulated it."

"Who is dealing with the Yorke family? Is that you, Caroline?"

"Yes, sir, I am their family liaison officer. They are dreadfully distressed, understandably, but they are being well supported by friends and family. I did pick up something from Mrs Yorke, however. She said something had been worrying him for the past few days, possibly things within the Mart. He said something was not right at all and he couldn't believe what he had found out. She said he had mentioned that someone who is educated and important should know better. He wouldn't tell her who or what because it would worry her. I asked why. She said she knew a few of his workmates but the only well-educated ones she could think of were the auctioneers, Mr Atkins, Mr William and Mr Ted and Mr William's son, and a few others, about three or four of them."

"Have we done checks on all of them, Fred?"

"Yes, all clean except one, a man called Harold Potter, would you believe? He had a conviction for criminal damage some years ago. I got the details. He was drunk, had a row over a girl and broke a window."

"Not quite in the same league but we will check him out. Anyone else got a theory? Yes, Chelsea?"

"I may be quite wrong, but do we know where Pickstaff was yesterday?"

"Good point, Tarik. Did you follow that up?"

"Yes. There was no reply at his home, so I got British Transport Police to check his duties on the railway. He's been on leave for three days and is booked for another two. As he rang in yesterday saying he wanted two more days as he was down in Swindon and then going to a place in Oxfordshire called Didcot, to a railway museum. The Cumbria police have some information on him; they are faxing it through to us and say he is known as being somewhat weird and moody. His neighbours have complained about him several times."

"I think we need to talk to him then. Fred, you have something else?"

"He is known in the red-light area of Leeds as well. They told me he is also a frequent visitor to the redlight area of Kings Cross in London. I have circulated him as being of interest."

"Des, you know these folks round here. Have you any ideas about what has happened?"

"Not really, sir. It is all so odd. I keep records, totally unofficial, of course. I didn't have time to look through them yesterday, but I do remember we had a bit of trouble over some stirks and the boundary between the Boothbys and their neighbours, the Goodyards. There was some sort of feud between them. Their lads had a falling-out, I think, over a girl about eighteen months ago or a bit longer. I had to speak to the Goodyards, the father, that is, as he had allegedly threatened to shoot young Boothby if he didn't get his animals back. Something to do with failing fences or fallen walls. He is a surly chap, Goodyard. None of his neighbours like him. He is a lazy farmer too, doesn't maintain anything."

"Wasn't he at the mart yesterday?"

"Yes, he apparently spoke to James Boothby when he first missed Colin."

"Then someone needs to see him."

"I think I had better do that, sir. He does not take kindly to strangers turning upon his farm. The footpath officer has been out there several times and had a run-in with him over a blocked footpath and some ramblers that he had covered in slurry when they wouldn't leave his land. If anyone turns up in Civi's, he is likely to kick off. He knows better than to threaten me."

"Has he form do you know?"

"Yes, a bit. He's been done for assault and years ago for GBH on his brother-in-law. I wasn't here then. Good yard told me the brother-in-law was cheating on this wife and needed sorting."

"Sounds a rather unpleasant chap. Take someone with you as well as Chelsea."

"I will, sir."

The meeting broke up and Saul occupied himself with administration matters and reading all the faxes and messages and the statements that were being brought in by the team. At about eight-thirty that evening, Chelsea and Des Trotter came into his office with Tarik Singh. Saul looked up and asked, "Any luck?"

"Yes and no, sir. He confirms James Boothby spoke to him and that he saw Colin in the morning, talking to Eric. Then he says Colin walked off towards the village with a bunch of flowers; yes, they were white roses. He noticed and asked Colin what they were for, but says Colin said nothing and walked off, but I don't believe him. I think they might have had words. He was most defensive. Surly chap. But Chelsea found something out."

"Yes, sir, while Des and Sergeant Singh were chatting to the father, the son came out and started chatting to me. He told me that Colin Boothby and he had met in The Bell the week before and even had a few pints together, and

71

Colin had told him he intended to go and see Mr Pickstaff and that he wanted to find something out about Alison, that had been worrying him."

"What else did he say?"

"He admitted that he, too, had been sweet on her, but the father had never even let him in their house, and every time she did go out, he got angry with her and even locked her in a couple of times. He told me quite a lot about Alison, actually."

"What kind of things?"

"He said she was very pretty even said I looked a lot like her, having blonde hair, blue eyes, same sort of height and build. He actually asked me out, but I said I was too busy."

Saul frowned and said, "Are you interested?"

"No way, sir. I am most definitely not interested. He is not my type, and he needs a good wash. He stank, mainly of BO, I think."

Des laughed and added, "The whole family are like that. They keep their animals in a bad state, too. The RSPCA got called last year, probably by the ramblers, but the whole place is a tip. The RSPCA visit quite often."

As Chelsea went to get her coat, Saul asked Des, "Just how like the dead girl is she?"

"Very, sir. From a distance, she could be her. Their facial features are a bit different but not greatly so. I'd not thought about it before, but I see the likeness now. I must admit I have been the envy of many officers since she arrived!"

"Yes, she is a beautiful woman. Look, I do not want Pickstaff to see her, not yet anyway. If he did kill his daughter, we might just need to unnerve him. and for that, she might be very useful if she is willing."

"I see; it did occur to me that she might be able to get young Boothby to talk; it might work."

"Good thinking. Tell me, will she be all right living with the Whales?"

"They will adore her, look after her, protect her and help her. From what she has told me about her family, I think she could do with a bit of that. She knows no one will help her. I must say I have been very impressed with how bright she is."

"So, have I. We must not put too much pressure on her."

"I know. My Missus likes her and has befriended her. My twelve-year-old son is awestruck and stares at her as if she is a goddess. She is very sweet to him. He is very moonstruck; I think it is his first crush. It is quite amusing; I have to tell him to shut his mouth and not gawp at her so much!"

"Poor lad! One of my sons had a crush like that on one of his teachers. It lasted all of a month. How is she coping with it?"

"Very well. She is aware of it and treats him like an adult, a friend. I do not think this is the first time it has happened to her. She is not vain or even aware of her beauty. She is very mature for her age."

When Chelsea got back to the farm, she found her bed made up, a fire lit and a note saying, **Meal in the farm**

kitchen for you. Do come in and we will be up till midnight.

She knocked on the kitchen door and Cyril got out of his chair by the fire and said, "Welcome, lass. Sit down, the meals in the oven. Bridget should be in any minute; she has gone to a WI meeting. Her friend drops her off at the gate. Have you had a good day?"

They chatted happily, together getting the meal ready on the table. Then Bridget came in, bearing a tray which Chelsea took for her while Cyril fetched in some bags. Bridget sighed and remarked, "Thanks, lass. I've brought some biscuits home and I won the raffle. It is a cushion what Mrs Utley made, patchwork, but I can't use it. The colours are all wrong. I can't put it back in the raffle, so I shall have to find another home for it unless you care for it?"

Chelsea looked at the cushion. It was beautifully made but was, in a variety of pink, puce, purple and mauve, and she agreed that it was definitely not her style at all. "Thank you, but it isn't my style either, but I do know someone who might be interested. This would fetch a bit where I used to work. I am sure someone will find it beautiful; it is rather striking and very modern."

"Well, it's too modern for me. You take it to them. I'll be glad to see the back of it. She is always making them, puts hours into it, she would like to sell them, I think."

"Then why don't I ask? Maybe they will give her an order? They are always looking for the unusual."

"She would be delighted. Now let's eat."

Saul was also home late. His wife Anna was waiting up for him. She asked, "Tired dear?"

"Very. What's wrong?"

"You always know, don't you? It's Ruth. They have let her out of hospital on a home visit. She rang me and said she wanted to meet up. I don't want to. I know she's my sister, but she scares me. She sounds fairly normal, but I could sense tension in her voice."

"Then don't. I certainly do not want her here again. I thought she had been told not to bother us?"

"She was, but she said as I was her sister, I owed it to her to hear her out. She also tried to ring the girls at their school but did not get through; the school rang me. It worries me."

"Have you spoken to the hospital?"

"Yes, I rang them. Her consultant is on holiday, and she was seen by a locum, who assures me she is all right. Last time I spoke to her usual consultant, he said she was not well at all and would be needing hospitalisation for some time, and asked me not to contact her, as she blames me and you for her being there."

"I will ring them in the morning."

"She told me, not asked, mind you, to be at her place at ten. When I said no, she slammed the phone down. What if she turns up here again?"

"She did enough damage last time. I wish I could be here, but I can't. I will ring Jake and see if he and Di can come."

"Thank you. Now, do you want the really bad news?"

"Go on, the only thing I can think of that is worse than your family turning up is if mine were too."

After a pause, he said, "When are they coming?"

"Abraham and Malachi are arriving on Friday. They say they have a service here at the synagogue on Saturday and they want you there."

"They would! I expect Malachi is preaching. He is getting almost as important as he thinks he is. I suppose I shall have to go. Where are they staying?"

"They assumed we would put them up. I could hardly say no."

"This is just getting better and better! We will have a thoroughly miserable weekend. Shall we run away and join a circus instead?"

Anna laughed. "No, we'll cope. I just hope they don't go on about evil gentiles and the holocaust again."

"When they are in our house, they will have to respect us. I'll ask Jake to come over with Diana. He can usually out-argue them; I just fold at the first theological hurdle."

"I'll get Kosha food in and hide the rest."

"I do love you, Anna. Wouldn't it be wonderful if we had normal relatives? Your sister is mentally ill, and my family are religious zealots or outlandish spies. I often wonder how our children are so well-adjusted. I'll get home as soon as I can tomorrow."

Saul rang his brother Jake and having spoken to him, put the phone down. "This week could be fun. They rang Jake and demanded he go to the synagogue too. He told them he would be delighted to. He's obviously up to something, I'm sure of it. He really dislikes Malachi."

Chapter 6

In the small hours of the morning, Saul and several others went to the exhumation of Alison Pickstaff's body. Later, with William Atkins, Junior and, Mrs Yorke and Saul made appeals at a press conference. Saul then went and opened inquests of both deaths and managed to get back to his office by lunchtime. He rang his home and was relieved when Jake answered, "Jake, any sign of Ruth?"

"Not yet, no. We did have an irate phone call from her demanding to know why Anna had not turned up, and I explained that she was otherwise occupied. Ruth began ranting at me, you know, the usual stuff she comes out with, so I let her rant on for a while and then just hung up. I got Di to take Anna out shopping. I'll deal with Ruth if she is stupid enough to turn up here. What time will you be home?"

"I don't know. I have to go to a PM, but I will get back as soon as I can."

Saul was on his way to the mortuary when he got a call on his mobile from his wife, Anna. As soon as he arrived, he asked the mortuary attendant, George, if he could use the phone there, as his battery was very low on the mobile.

George, who had known him for many years, opened the door to the office and said, "What is wrong? Can I help, Mr Catchpole?"

"My wife has hit a problem and I need to talk to her." George discreetly withdrew and shut the office door behind him.

"Anna, what has happened?"

"I went shopping with Di. I bought something and the floor manager of the big department store came back and said, Mrs Diana Catchpole? Of course, we both said yes and then we found out it was me he wanted. He explained that the bank card I had given him had been reported stolen and had been cancelled and the bank had instructed him to cut it up. I rang the bank who told me I had reported it stolen this morning, so Di paid for me. We went round to the bank and saw the manager. He said I had rung him and told him all my cards had been stolen and he had, therefore, stopped them; I explained I had done no such thing. Di was able to say she had been with me at the time the call had been made, which was ten sixteen, and I had made no such call."

"It was Ruth?"

"It had to be. We do sound quite similar. Then I asked if your card had been reported stolen, too. He looked it up and said that two of them had. I trust you have not used them?"

"Which two?"

"Our joint account and your main one."

"Both of which I had when Ruth last visited. I wonder what else she has details of."

"Can you do a check on my car, and I suppose yours as well?"

"Leave that with me. Where are you now?"

"In Di's car heading to the cinema."

Saul made several calls to banks, his control room and leaving enough money to cover the cost of the calls on the desk left the office. George was waiting in the corridor.

"Everything all right, sir?"

"Not really. Thanks for the use of the phone. My wife's sister is mentally ill and is trying to cause trouble for both of us. She has reported my bank cards, my wife's bankcards, our cars and one or two other things stolen. I think I have sorted it, but I am wondering what else she has up her sleeve."

"That is vicious. Can I help in any way? Look, I'll get you a coffee. They have just started the first PM."

The examination of Alison Pickstaff's body was most revealing. She was remarkably well preserved. The pathologist could find no trace of heart damage consistent with any kind of infection and no other signs of illness. They could only wait for toxicology results to establish a cause of death, but it was suspicious as there were signs of injection marks on the back of her neck. Saul rang the results through and then drove home. He pulled into his road just as a woman was approaching his front door. It was his sister-in-law, Ruth. He quickly called for police assistance and leaving his car out of sight, followed her up the drive and said, "What do you want, Ruth? You know you are not welcome here."

As she swung round to speak to him, Jake opened the front door and stood firmly in the doorway.

"I want to see my sister Diana."

"Well, Anna does not want to see you. She asked you not to contact her, but you did. She has gone out. Why did you report her car and her bank cards stolen? That was a pretty mean thing to do."

"I'll make her talk to me. If that is the only way I can get her attention, I'll go on until she does talk to me. She does not even answer my letters."

"I know she didn't want to. I saw what you said to her in them. You are ill, Ruth and until you are well again, which you obviously are not, leave us alone, please. You have caused enough trouble and distress already. Please do not be in any doubt; I will protect my wife and family."

"But I am her elder sister; she must talk to me."

"Not if everything you say causes unhappiness. Either leave now or wait until you are arrested. Either way, leave my property; you are trespassing."

Ruth snarled at him, and her expression was one of pure hatred. "You foul Jews. It's all your fault. You stole my sister, who is called Diana, not Anna like you say, and then got me locked up in a mental institution with a load of foul lies. I hate you and I will make you pay. You just wait!"

With a manic laugh, she pushed past him and went out onto the road and looked around, but unable to find his car stood screeching obscenities at him and Jake.

Saul and Jake listened, as did many of their neighbours. Saul said quietly to Jake, "It's all right. Help is on the way. She is arrestable. Did Di tell you what she did?"

"Yes. How come they let her out?"

"Some locum fell for her. I'm sane, really, act. The hospital told me that her notes state she must not be released."

Before long, a police car arrived and took Ruth, who was still screeching threats and abuse, away. While they waited for their wives to return, Saul made a coffee and then asked, "What are you going to the synagogue for, Jake? What are you up to?"

"I want to hear that pious, bigoted little creep of a nephew of ours speak. I wondered what he had to say. I may have left our faith, but I still know a fair bit about it."

"You know Abe is not that bad."

"He is awful, Saul; he has put Malachi on a pedestal and thinks the sun shines out of his bum. Abe is a bit obsessed with tradition and his son's notoriety and has become a total bore on the subject."

"Come on, Jake, Abe used to be fun, remember? He was a great little brother. Do tell me, have they had the pleasure of meeting Diana yet?"

"No, they have not. They know little about her. I will be very interested to see what they think. It might just take the pressure off Anna for a while. Di can look after herself."

"Don't I know it!"

"While we are waiting for our wives to return, shall we get drunk?"

"No, that will not help. Coffee is fine."

Not long after, Anna and Di pulled in and unloaded purchases from their car. The men went to help, and both flinched at the apparent cost of the purchases. Then, they had a pleasant evening together.

Anna asked, "Did Ruth turn up?"

Saul smiled and said, "Yes and was taken away. Which reminds me, I must ring the hospital."

Just as he was about to return to the lounge, he took a call from his Detective Inspector Bickerstaff. He then returned to the lounge.

"I have to go into work early tomorrow. They have picked up one of my suspects and I need to interview him. I doubt he is the murderer but there are a number of things we need to talk to him about."

Di said, "Yes, I saw the press conference. That poor woman that lost her husband. What is this all about?"

"Yes, Mrs Yorke, a lovely woman. I think her husband discovered something. He was at the wrong place at the wrong time. It is a strange case and at the moment, I cannot discover a real motive."

"Would it help to talk it through?"

"It might, yes."

They sat in the lounge with a good bottle of wine, and Saul said, "I have two dead men, one seriously injured, and exhumed body of a girl that died a year ago. That we now believe was murdered. They are all closely connected to the farming community. I think it is about love, jealousy, revenge and desire, but it could be something else. There is a shoal of red herrings. One of the neighbouring farmer's sons was sweet on the same girl that the lad who was injured wanted to marry. This lad turned up miles away and then we have a lorry load of sheep that were just dumped on a moor, and an employee of the auction mart that we have just picked up, that we know is a burglar, not to mention his having an intimate knowledge of where the bodies were found. The father of the dead girl is apparently on holiday, taken at the last minute. Then we have the interesting fact that some dogs did not bark in the night, some flowers on a grave, not to mention a missing sheep transporter that turned up miles away."

"This sounds very complicated. Are you sure it is all connected?"

"Not sure, no, Jake. I think what happened was the injured lad went to visit the grave of his dead fiancée. He met someone there and had an argument with them or a fight, and then went back to the auction mart, which is not far away, and was either followed or met someone who was hit over the head and put into the sheep transporter. This was either before or after the driver of the transporter was murdered and hidden. Poor Herbert Yorke was either a witness or tried to stop it and was killed to shut him up. And then his body was hidden. The sheep in the transporter were then driven away and later, the sheep and the injured lad were dumped over in Littondale. The empty vehicle was dumped not far from a main road."

"Who would have wanted to kill the lorry driver?"

"He had a very bad reputation with women. He was a potential rapist. Everything else could slot into place if he was not involved. He was killed by having his head bashed in. The lad had his head bashed, but Herbert Yorke had his throat cut."

"Do you know how the girl died?"

"Not yet, toxicology might tell us."

"Who do you think killed her then?"

"What I think and what I can prove are very different. Her father, if you must know. I think the lad, Colin, had found out something wasn't right and maybe the father followed him. I just can't work out how the lorry driver fits in."

"Did this lorry driver know the dead girl?"

"I have no reason to think so, Di, but I will check."

"Why would a father kill his own daughter?"

"He didn't want her seeing anyone. Apparently, he made her a virtual prisoner. He was very controlling."

"No wife or siblings?"

"Not that I know of."

"Has he remarried? Maybe there is a stepmother?"

"I don't know."

Anna said, "What was the girl's name? Maybe she went to the school I taught at near there?"

"Alison Pickstaff."

"Yes, I remember her. Beautiful blonde child; we suspected she was being abused when she was in her second year. She lived with her father; her mother had died. He was a railway worker, if I remember. She was one of a trio of girls, a Debbie and a Bernadette. They were all very good at sports and played hockey for the school, I remember. Debbie Totton, that was her name and Bernadette came from a large family, O'Dwyer, and her father was a builder. Staunch Catholics, I believe. I taught them all at some stage. One girl in the family became a nun; another lad went into the priesthood; another girl became an air hostess. Bernadette, unfortunately, went the wrong way. I saw her conviction in the paper for soliciting not long ago."

The next morning, Saul attended the reburial of Alison and had arranged for the local vicar to be there to give a blessing. He then went into the office armed with a lot more information. He collected Tarik and together they went to the cell block and interviewed Norman Ley. Saul soon thought the lad was clever but also very sly. Norman happily admitted the burglaries and living in the basement of the auction mart. He agreed he knew all about the underground pipes and the drainage system. He happily admitted all the thefts within the building. When he was asked about the murders, he was not so forthcoming.

"No way, I didn't do them. The reason I took off when they happened was, I didn't want you lot questioning me. I wasn't the only person using those pipes, you know. Someone else was. I never saw them like, but I knew there was someone doing it. Scared me to death at first, but when I realised, they must know about me and have said nothing, I relaxed a bit."

"Did you steal the angle grinder to cut through the bars?"

"I took the grinder, yes, but the bars had already been cut through, I think, with a hacksaw. I needed to trim them off. Whoever did it would have been a bit slimmer than me."

"How did you find out about the tunnels?"

"I was going through the bins. You can sometimes find one or two bits worth salvaging. There was an old newspaper in there, opened at a page about this young girl who died in them. It was from the auctioneer's office; that is the first I look at. I found a good pen there once that I got a bit of money for."

"When was this?"

"Some time ago. Mr William, he'd asked me to help move some furniture and that. Old Mr Atkins he'd moved offices the previous week. The younger auctioneers then moved into what had been Mr Williams's office."

"Tell me, Norman, this other person that was using the tunnels, did they ever leave anything?"

"They might have."

"Do you know who it is?"

"I've got an idea; what is it worth for me to tell you?"

Saul sighed and then explained, "I don't do deals; you are in a lot of trouble already, Norman."

"OK, okay. I'm not sure, mind, but I think I know; it really surprised me."

"Did anyone suspect you or this other person?"

"Herbert started asking questions about the basement."

"Why?"

"He knew someone was using it. He sort of warned me off about it. Said it could be dangerous."

"Who else knows about the tunnels?"

"Mickey, I think Herbert, Mr William, and his dad, of course, and the brother who lives over in Hawes. You asked me if this person left anything. He did once. It was a little pouch-type thing, I looked in it and it had pills in there, two different types, not anything I knew about; I left them alone, but I did look them up. It is something you take for a thing called Angina, whatever that is. I left them where I found them, and they had gone the next day."

"Were you staying there most nights?"

"No, only when I had nowhere else to go. I've got this girl; see, when her parents have gone to bed, I sneak into her room."

"So, who is this other person? If you are honest with us, Norman, I can say that you have been helpful."

"All right, whoever it is, is slimmer than me, which ain't many. I know they wear a grey suit. I found a piece of grey material snagged on one of the bars once. They have recently cut themselves on the jagged bit of the bar and there is blood there, not a lot. They keep a torch hidden just by the entrance. I never use it, got my own headset. I'll show you if you like."

"So, who is it?"

"I think it is Mr William's brother, Mr Ted. It doesn't make sense because he has his own set of keys. Either that or it could be that Mr Potter. He's slim enough, too. I think it is Mr Ted. He's been giving me weird looks recently like he knows. He said something that made me think. We were talking about rats 'cos we had the rat catcher in. Mr Ted was over for a big sale what was on. He said it wasn't just rats we needed to catch, and sometimes they could be quite big, and the big ones should be careful they don't get caught in a trap or find and entrance blocked or something. He was staring right at me when he said it."

"How often does he come over?"

"Too often. But about once a week. He is a bit weird. He wears a grey suit and had a new one recently."

"The day the bodies were found, where did you run off to?"

"When I saw you, lot arriving, I didn't want to hang around. I don't like coppers and PC Trotter doesn't like me much, so I went to the gents and slipped out of the window, legged it away, and caught the bus to Skipton. I went to my girlfriend's; she works at a burger bar. I had to pull Mickey out of the window, too."

"But you came back."

"How did you know that?"

"You were seen."

"All right, I did. OK, I hid for a while and then took my Land Rover and drove off. You lot were everywhere. I picked Mickey up down by the river bridge, and we went into Skipton. I dropped him off later. I hid the car for ages. I heard about Herbert and knew you lot would want to talk to me, well, all of us what was there. I'm really sorry about Herbert; he was a nice chap, kind like. I didn't like Eric, though."

"Why not?"

"He was right slimy; thought he was a real ladies' man. Ugly git kept trying to touch the girls up. He upset Lisa and Debbie that I do know."

"When you were hanging around keeping out of our way, did you see anything odd or unusual?"

"Sort of. First, Mr Ted drove into the car park, but after a couple of minutes, he drove off again. I think when he saw a police car there. Then Mr Potter came in minutes later and did the same thing. After I had picked Mickey up, we drove down that road to Rathmell and I saw this big fat bloke. I don't remember seeing him before. There was a car parked just down there in a lay-by. It was a blue Peugeot estate, dark blue. I watched in my mirror and saw him get into it and sit in the driver's seat. I can even tell you the number, GWR1T. I remember it because I reckon it must have cost a bit."

"Did you see Eric drive a sheep transporter out?"

"Yes, sure I did. Bert gave him the papers and once they had loaded the sheep, they were hogs. Actually, I saw him drive off, I nipped out for a fag and I saw Eric stop the lorry out in the far lorry park and he got out and was hanging around waiting for someone. I finished my fag and came back in."

"Did you see or pass anyone going that way?"

"Sure, I did. I wondered which one was going to meet him. First of all, there was Mr William. I hid from him as it was not my break time. Then there was Lisa from the canteen and Debbie from the office; I think they were going to have a fag too. There were several farmers; I don't know all their names but one of them was that surly bastard whose sheep are always so dirty. Mr Shityard, we call him. I heard some'at about him recently; I was listening to talk in the corridor outside the canteen. He's got a daughter;

she's quite pretty. She is fourteen or fifteen, and she goes to the same special school as my little sister does. Shityard has brought her here several times when he is at the auction. I heard that she got pregnant by one of the drivers, probably Eric. Shityard had been there all day. He came back in from outside later, and next time when I went out, the transporter had gone. I saw Colin's father looking for his lad a bit later. He must have passed Shityard when he went out."

"What is Shityard's real name?"

"I dunno, it is something yard. I know his first name is Robbie. If I tell you what it is worth?"

"It rather depends on how truthful and helpful you are."

"I'll tell you something else then. That lad what went missing, Colin, he was wandering round with a bunch of white roses earlier. Looked a right pratt. He came back later without them. He looked rather upset, so I asked what the matter was. And if he was okay. He said he needed to think something out and needed to make a phone call. I said the cattle ring wasn't being used. He said thanks and went down to the cattle ring, and I saw him go in and sit down. I had to go and load some calves then, so I left him to it."

"Did you see anyone else go into the cattle ring?"

"Not that I saw, no. I didn't say owt because I would have got into trouble, and I was supposed to be helping with the calves. There was something I thought was a bit odd, though. I like to know what is going on; yes, I know I'm nosey. When I was hanging around later to get my

Land Rover, I went over to where that sheep lorry had been. I noticed a bit of piping with shit and stuff on it and what looked like blood. Like someone had killed a sheep or something, I kicked it into the bushes. Come to think of it; there was a bit of three by two there as well, that was from our wood store. In with the spare hurdles."

"Will you show us?"

"If you like. I never touched them; I just kicked them away."

Saul and Tarik got some more details and left, having returned Norman to his cell. Other officers were dealing with the burglaries and thefts and were waiting to interview him. As they left the station, Tarik said, "That car number is Pickstaff's car, I think?"

"Yes, I believe so. Just how much of that do you think is true?"

"Most of it. He is pretty bright; it's a pity he is not honest as well. I am not sure about Mr Ted; that doesn't make sense. Why would a man with keys and lawful access to a building, apparently with a heart complaint, want to sneak in and out? What would be the point?"

"He doesn't want anyone to know he's been there. I suspect the alarm system records who access and when; I need to talk to old Mr Atkins, who has, in fact, asked me to visit him."

Chapter 7

The next morning, while the rest of the team followed up on the many enquiries, Saul drove out to a beautiful and rather large house a few miles from the Mart in the countryside. As he approached the front door, a gentleman came out, introduced himself as Mr Atkins and ushered him into an elegant drawing room and produced tea and biscuits.

He said, "Chief Superintendent, please sit down. Thank you so much for coming; I need to talk to you. My sons, bless them, think they are protecting me by telling me as little as possible just because I have a dickey heart; they think my mind is gone, too. I want to know what is going on."

"So, do I. I think you may be able to help me with several things."

Saul told him as much as he could about what they had learned so far. After another cup of tea, Mr Atkins said, "Fire away, man, what do you want to know? It must be about my family; why else would you come out here to see me? They can tell you about the business; I only go in part-time now."

"Yes, one of the things I need to ask you about stems from the tragic death of your daughter years ago."

"Yes, that was ghastly. I always blame myself. Most of it came out at the inquest; that is a matter of public record, which no doubt you have already looked at. Yes, I thought so. Will was not involved; it was Ted and Alice. Alice was the older one; she was supposed to be looking after Ted. They went off to play. They had a real squabble, quite a scrap. I had just given them their pocket money and told them they could go down to the shop if they wanted to get some sweets. When they came back, Ted had spent all his money, but Alice had not. He said he wanted an ice cream, but she would not buy him one. He was going through a very naughty stage. I told them to behave and find somewhere quiet to play. Then they went off together and we discovered they were missing a while later. We searched, I mean everyone did, even those attending the auction, and eventually someone heard him calling and we found them under the grill of the saw tank. Ted was hanging onto the grill, yelling his head off, so we prized it up and pulled both of them out. Alice was not conscious and was rushed to hospital and Ted followed. He was okay after getting over the shock and cold but she was not. She died in hospital later that day. It broke my wife's heart. Ted stayed in hospital for a couple of days. He told us he had slipped and fallen in and couldn't get to her in time. He told us he had pulled her up but couldn't get her to talk. He went on to explain they had found this large pipe and she had suggested they explore it. He was taller than her; she was rather small for her age. That's about it. He became quiet, withdrawn and very introverted for a long time. The coroner questioned him, of course and was very gentle with him."

"Did you ask him what had happened?"

"Of course, we did. He didn't want to talk about it to me or my wife. He changed after that. We had a lot of problems with him; he was naughty at school and disruptive. He began being very difficult with my wife. We got him all sort of help and eventually, he grew out of it."

"Did he ever speak about it after that?"

"Not to me. Just before Biddie, my wife died some years ago, she told me something. She said she never believed his story and that she didn't think he had changed much. She confessed to me that all along, she thought he had pushed her into that tank in a temper. She had never wanted to know the truth because he was her son, and she couldn't voice her suspicions, not even to me."

"What do you believe now?"

"He is a strange man. I know he's my son, but he has always been jealous of Will. I saw him push Will off his bike quite deliberately once. When he was a teenager, Ted was so envious of Will that we had to send them to different schools. Will always looked out for Ted, defended him to the hilt and tried to look after him, but I know that Ted really hurt Will several times. Since they have grown up, we have managed to keep them far enough apart for things to be civilised."

"Did Ted want to come into the business?"

"Not initially, no. He went to university and then joined the army, but came out as soon as he could. I was quite surprised when he qualified and then asked to come into the family firm, especially considering that he always said he hated the lot of us before he went to university. I thought he resented being a junior partner. We were thinking of promoting him next year."

"Does he, by any chance, suffer from angina?"

"Yes, now how would you know that? Like me, he is cursed with it. He hasn't had it long. He has always been so fit. He runs and cycles a lot. He always was a skinny lad. But strong and wiry. Will is built more like me. He, thankfully, does not have angina, yet anyway."

"Who deals with the financial side of the firm?"

"I did, but Ted took over last year. He qualified in accountancy."

"Have you had an audit recently?"

"No, the annual one is overdue; why?"

"I just wondered."

"No, you think something is going on. Come on out with it, man, be straight with me; I'm not a fool; I have told you about Ted. You may not suspect him of anything, but I do. I always have. Sad, isn't it? He asked to take on the financial side of things and said he was rather underemployed over at the Hawes branch. If you ask that question, there was a reason; I think it might be prudent to get that audit done as soon as possible, tomorrow, say?"

"I have no evidence, but I have reason to believe that he may have been using the old drain to get into the mart building. As he has keys, I can only think he does not want it known he has been there. I understand your alarm system records all entries. Does he have a family?"

"No, and never will. I am afraid our Ted bats for the other side. He hated his mother and I think Alice too. He seems to hate all women. That is why he left the army because he is gay. He does have a relationship, however. One of the younger auctioneers is that way inclined, I believe, young Potter. Slimy little chap, I don't like him, but I have to admit he is good at the job. My sons think I don't know what goes on, but I have eyes behind my specs and my hearing is quite adequate. The only reason I can think he wouldn't want anyone knowing he was there is if he was cooking the books. I will set that audit in motion. Ted has put it off by three months already. I used to do the finances and I know it was all in order when I handed it over to him. His excuse was that he needed the extra time to change it to the computers. I am still in charge of the company, at least. I will tell you I am really upset about Herbert Yorke. His father worked for me for years and so did Herbert. Have you a number I can contact you on?"

Saul handed Mr Atkins his card and added, "If you are worried, you can ring me any time. I may be quite wrong. Did you know Potter has a conviction?"

"Yes, we did. It was some time ago and we decided to give him a second chance."

Saul said, "This is a beautiful house. Do you live here alone?"

"No, I have a wing here. Will and his family live in the main part of the house. Since my wife passed on, I am grateful for their company and my grandchildren are a great joy. I play a bit of golf and am busy with one or two societies; I keep pretty active."

The conversation became a bit more general and then Saul mentioned how helpful Bridgett had been.

"She is a gem! I was so sorry they could never have children. She and her husband are lovely people. I knew her mother years back. She was a nurse; you know, one of those old-fashioned sisters, terrifying but wonderful."

"Bridget must take after her mother then. I got a small cut on my hand and confronted her. I knew better than to argue, so I meekly complied with instructions!"

"Wise man! She has run that office like clockwork for years. I got hit by a marauding pig once when we sold pigs, and she patched me up. She accused me of being a baby when I complained it was hurting,"

"Me too. One of my young women officers is lodging with her!"

"Lucky girl, she will be smothered, mothered and looked after so well I doubt she will ever move on."

Saul found Mr Atkins excellent company, and when he left, he knew that the audit would begin the next day. After the case was over, he fully intended to take up Mr Atkins's offer of friendship. He drove to the auction mart and found William Atkins at his desk in his office.

Mr William beckoned him in and said, "Hello, now how can I help you? I must say your officers are a tidy lot. They have taken great care and left things immaculate. Do sit down, please. Would you like a coffee while we chat? I'll get one fetched in. I think you want to talk to me, so I'll shut the door."

Saul told him what he could about how the case was going and then said, "The day the bodies were found, did you go out the back car park about lunchtime?"

"Yes, I'd forgotten. I went over to see the computer dealer who rents the building there. I had hoped he could help me understand something. Computers are not my forte! He wasn't there, but his secretary told me he would get back to me."

"May I ask what it was you couldn't understand?"

"Yes, of course. It was how to get into our main account. Ted has changed it all to internet banking. I'd rung Ted but he was out. The office at Hawes said they didn't know where he was. I never seem to have trouble paying things into the account, but I tried to take a small amount out and couldn't. It just froze on me every time I tried. So, I wrote a cheque instead from my personal account. Thanks for reminding me; I will sort that with Ted."

"Did you see a sheep transporter in the car park?"

"Not that I can remember, but I cannot honestly say there was not one there; they often gather to leave in a convoy."

"Who else did you see?"

"Let me think, yes, Norman Ley was there, having a sneaky fag, I think he thought I hadn't spotted him. Lisa and Debbie, I suspect doing the same and a couple of farmers."

"Can you remember who?"

"There was Paul Hickman; I saw he had a new four-by-four, Sam Hewitt and his new wife. Stephen Oldman was just leaving and yes, Mr Goodyard. I don't think there was anyone else."

"Thank you. Where might I find your brother, Edward?"

"He works from the Hawes office. He has not been here for at least a fortnight. I can ring him if you like?"

"He was here briefly the day we found the bodies. He drove into the car park and then out again."

"He didn't tell me that. When I rang him yesterday, he said he had not been here. He also mentioned that young Potter had not either."

"Well, Potter was here that day, too. He drove in and out of the car park without stopping."

"Oh, I see. I can tell you what that is about then. They probably agreed to meet here. They think I don't know about them. My brother is gay, you see, and so is Potter. So long as it hurts no one, I don't care about it."

"Thanks, but why would he lie to you?"

"It won't be the first time. Ted and I don't get on. Unfortunately, I have to work with him but there is little love lost between us."

"Why?"

"It is a jealousy thing. I was the eldest boy, and he has always resented it. We had quite a falling out when my mother died. She had left me some things, jewellery for my wife and daughters. He wanted it. She had left him quite a bit of money, more than the jewellery was worth, I think. I don't know why he wanted it; it is not like he will use it. I suspect it was simply because I had it and he did not."

"I see. Maybe I'll run up to Hawes and speak to him there, see if he saw anyone here that day."

"Well, I know he is not in the office today; I understand he is at some meeting or other to do with the Rotary. As a matter of fact, he was not at the Hawes office that day either or any of our other offices, Leyburn or Clitheroe."

"I'll leave it until tomorrow then. Where does he live?"

"Just outside Hawes, I'll give you, his details."

Chapter 8

A couple of days later, Chelsea and Des had a day off. Chelsea was about to go into town and popped in to see Bridget.

"I'm going into town. Do you want to come with me?"

"I would love to; what had you in mind?"

"I was going to get some colour charts and some curtain material and some cloth samples so I can redecorate the annexe for you."

"You can do your place up how you like; you know."

"You said, but it is your place, and you should choose how it is done. Come on, I'll buy you lunch; I think you have the day off, too?"

They spent a splendid morning and had a good lunch at The Lamb pub before heading back.

Chelsea asked, "Do you mind if I just pop in and leave a message for Des? I won't be long."

"Not at all, dear, I'm fine. I like these colours here; this aqua colour would be good for our bathroom."

A few minutes later, Chelsea came out of Des' house with Mrs Trotter and a gangly boy who thrust a bunch of flowers into Chelsea's hands as she left. They were a pretty posy of wildflowers; Chelsea thanked him and got into the car.

Bridget held the flowers and said, "You've made a hit there. How old is he?"

"Twelve, it is very sweet, if a bit embarrassing. He'll soon get over it."

"Poor lad, does this happen a lot to you?"

"Just occasionally."

"Do you have a gentleman friend?"

"Not at the moment, and I am not actually looking for one."

"I am sure you must have the pick of who you want?"

"I have a career to concentrate on at the moment. I am sure I will find the right man in time."

"You mean when you are ready, not like that man who stared at you and followed us in town?"

"Yes, that was a bit weird when we went to the shop just down from the railway station. I thought he was a bit creepy, and I was ever so glad you were with me. It was almost as though he thought he knew me, and I was grateful we could keep our distance."

"I've seen him somewhere before, but I can't place him. It could be at the auction mart, I suppose. I know I have met him; it'll come to me."

"It's not important. Now, do you want me to ring Mrs Uttley and ask if she is interested in selling those cushions she makes? My old firm liked that one and, as you heard, offered her a good price. I'll get the room cleared and make a start in the bedroom."

When Aileen Trotter told Des about the flowers, he laughed and said, "Oh dear, I am afraid that might be my fault. He asked me this morning how to court a woman. I told him I gave you flowers sometimes and he went off to count his pocket money from his piggy bank. I said not to waste good money and it was the thought that counted. Are you worried about it?"

"No, I think it is rather sweet. She was very kind and did not do anything to encourage him. Oh, Mrs Payne came in to see you earlier and says she thinks she has some information for you. Can you go and see her?"

"So much for a day off; I'll go there now. What did Chelsea want?"

"She left a note, something you asked her to do for you?"

The Murder Squad office manager, Fred Dunlop, was having a very bad day. Not only was it very busy but his MS had come out of remission, and he was feeling poorly. He kept dropping things. Saul came into the office just as Fred had dropped a pile of papers.

"Fred, are you feeling all right?"

"No, guv'nor 'm not. I'm having one of my bad days, feeling a bit rough."

"Then go home! You know we understand. You should be resting, saving your strength."

"I can't; there is too much to do."

"Then I will do it. Go home and that is an order! I'll call in someone else if we need it. We knew this would sometimes happen and I am quite prepared for it. I'll ring Paddy and 1 will also get someone to run you home and take your car back for you."

When Fred had gone, Saul rang Paddy, who had been deputising for Fred; Paddy was on rest day, so Saul wondered if he might have to find someone else.

Saul explained, and Paddy said he was free and would be in the office in half an hour. Saul then started sorting through the tray. He distributed posts for various squad members and noticed four sealed envelopes addressed to Chelsea. He put the post in the allocated places and then looked up to see a young, uniformed PC put another envelope in the in-tray, addressed to Chelsea. Saul said, "She is not in today. Was it urgent? Is it to do with a case?"

The young man blushed and said, "No, sir, I was just asking her out. I met her in the canteen yesterday and I think I'm in love!"

Saul smiled and said, "Well, I will put it in her tray, but I won't have her distracted from her job, mind."

"No, sir, of course not, sir."

The lad scurried off down the corridor and Saul chuckled to himself. He put the note in Chelsea's tray and noticed at least another dozen or so sealed and handwritten envelopes. He collected his post and spent some time reading through it.

Paddy turned up quite soon and Saul breathed a sigh of relief. "Paddy, thanks so much for coming in. I'd almost forgotten how much work there is just sorting through the results, not to mention other things. I have a lot of forensic results here. Will you help me go through them?"

When they had finished that, Saul asked, "Young Chelsea seems to have quite a following. Are they worrying her?"

"I don't think so. She glances at the notes and puts them away and does not do anything with them until she heads home. We have had a constant stream of amorous young men and some not-so-young calling here on a number of pretexts. If she isn't there, they go away most dejected. It is quite funny."

"Maybe not for her. Can you see how she feels about it?"

"I will ask her. I did warn off a couple of our more mature lotharios that are married and should know better."

"Good; if anyone becomes a pest, tell me and I will put a stop to it."

"I will, sir. Oh, look, here is the toxicology report for Alison Pickstaff. Look at a vast amount of digitalis, apparently injected into the back of the thigh. A highly lethal dose, murder definitely."

"Let's get moving on it then. Could you circulate the father as wanted, please?"

"Yes, of course, but wait, this report says that she was about four months pregnant. They have sent DNA samples off, so we might be able to identify the father. Oh, and a message has just come in for you from a Mr Atkins."

Saul read the message and said, "Interesting. Now I have to go and swear out some warrants for several things. You do know I am not in on Saturday? I will execute one of these warrants tomorrow, but I hope you and Geoff and Alan will hold the fort until I come back in."

The next morning, Saul was shown into the office of Mr Ted Atkins at the Hawes auction mart by a rather sour-faced woman.

Ted Atkins said to her as they came into the office, "Back to your work, Margaret! What do you want, officer?"

Saul felt the hairs on the back of his neck rise and a shiver ran down his spine. The presence of Ted Atkins was almost as overpowering as the aftershave he was wearing.

"I hoped you could help me by answering a few questions, Mr Atkins. As you know, I am investigating the murder of two men at the Skipton branch."

"Well, I was nowhere near it, so I cannot help you. Hurry up, please; as you can see, the office is very busy."

"Is it normally this busy?"

"No. The auditors are here. It is most inconvenient. For some reason, my senile father has decided to do a spot check. I need to go out, so can we get on?"

"That is one thing I wished to talk to you about the spot check."

"I thought you were from the Murder Squad."

"I am, but it is my duty to investigate whatever comes to my attention. Do you know what the auditors are looking for?"

"My father should have retired years ago. He cannot let go and obviously, this murder thing has made him flip. He clearly doesn't trust me."

"Has he any reason to mistrust you?"

"Of course not!"

"Then why are you so worried about the auditors?"

106

"They are a nuisance, taking up time and space."

"Very well. Let's talk about the death of your sister, Alice."

"I would rather not. It was a long time ago and I have tried to block it out of my memories. It has nothing to do with you, anyway."

"I do understand it must be painful for you. What I want to know is why you have been visiting the Skipton branch via the drainage pipes and ventilation shafts recently."

"Who said I had?"

"We have good reason believe it. Medications that you take have been found there and various bits of material and some blood have been found that may place you there."

"Don't be stupid; I have keys to the place; why would I not use them if I wished to visit?"

"Yes, I wondered that. I can think of several reasons, but I would rather you told me."

"Well, I deny it. Nor do I have any intention of giving you samples or my clothes, so that is your problem."

"What a pity; it could eliminate you if what you say is true. How much do you know about these murders?"

"Not much, only what my brother told me. I have not been there in over three weeks."

"Not even in the car park?"

"No. I do most of my business on the phone."

"So, you didn't drive into the car park there on Thursday the twelfth?"

"No. I just told you. Are you deaf or stupid, or both?"

"I heard what you said, but I don't believe you. You were seen there that day. You didn't stop, but you were there."

"Prove it. Now, unless you have any other impertinent questions, I have to go out."

"I have not finished yet. I need to serve this on you. It is a copy of the search warrant currently being executed at your house."

"That's outrageous. How dare you?"

"No, is called the lawful execution of a warrant. I had hoped you wanted to cooperate but as you will not, I have no other choice but to arrest you. I am arresting you on suspicion of fraud and false accounting."

Saul cautioned Atkins, who was going very white and glared at him, "That won't be necessary. All right, what do you want to know?"

"I'll ask you at the police station when you have been given all your rights. My officers are waiting outside. If I have your word not to try and escape, I will not handcuff you but know if you do run, you will be caught and restrained. Don't you want to bring your briefcase?"

"No, there's nothing important in it."

"Other than an air ticket to Spain from Manchester airport this afternoon and your passport?"

"That is my property, and you can't touch it."

"Yes, I can. I also have a warrant for here Mr Atkins, please think carefully. Whatever it is you have done or have not done will soon be apparent. I will take the briefcase, thank you."

The briefcase was locked, and Saul had to pull it from Ted Atkins's grip. Atkins was surprisingly strong.

Saul said, "I think we have been here before. Last time, you hit me with a lump of wood. Give up, man. I have only to call and the officers in the next room will come to my aid. When we struggled before, I managed to get a part of your jacket."

"I got the better of you then and can again. No, I will not come willingly, you arrogant bastard. Keep out of what does not concern you. I am no murderer."

"That we will have to investigate. If you wish to be dragged kicking and fighting to the police van, then so be it. I am giving you the opportunity to maintain a bit of dignity."

"Bugger dignity! Yes, all right, I was there but I didn't kill anybody."

"I think you might know who did, though."

"I am saying nothing more. Call your heavies in; I shall deny saying anything to you. It's only your word against mine. If I have an angina attack, it will be down to you."

"That is one reason I have tried to be civilised about this."

Atkins turned and picked up the substantial brass statuette of a bull from the desk and swung it at Saul. Saul was ready and neatly ducked and went to disarm Atkins but had to let go of the briefcase, which Atkins grabbed and flung through a window which shattered. Several officers rushed in and restrained and handcuffed Atkins and took him out of the room, struggling violently.

Then two other officers came in, and Saul asked them, "Did you hear it all?"

"Yes, sir, all recorded. Are you all right?"

"Yes, fine, thanks; how are we going to get that briefcase back?"

They looked out of the window and saw the briefcase lying on a flat roof below them. Saul looked at his two very hefty colleagues and said, "I'll get it. I am lighter than you two. Just help me down and then up again. Once we have it, I want your team to search thoroughly, including all computer records. We know there is a large sum of money missing, so any keys need to be found."

Saul, for all his slight limp, made light work of collecting the briefcase, handing it up to the two officers and before he came back up to join them, he looked around the flat roof. He saw a length of wood lying just under the window and with gloves, he picked it up and passed it up to them, noticing several strands of fibre on one end of it that looked like those missing from the suit he had been wearing the day of the murders.

The two officers pulled him back up into the office and then one received a message on his radio and then said, "We have his car keys, and they are searching for car now, or rather, scenes of crime are. I'll take this lump of wood to them."

Saul brushed himself off and then said, "Can you make sure that odious man has his medication available and make sure a police surgeon is at the station. He is that desperate. I wondered if he resisted bringing on an angina attack."

As they searched the room, another officer came in, "The keys we found on him, and there is a briefcase key on here, sir. Do you want to open it now?"

"Yes, let's see what it was he didn't want us to find, shall we?"

Inside the briefcase, there was an airline ticket that Saul noticed was first class, three passports, one in Atkins' name, one in Potters', and another in a different name but with Atkins' photo in. Then they saw the bundles of notes, mostly in Euros but also some in American dollars. At the bottom of the briefcase, Saul found several bottles of tablets which were labelled and others with no labels and with a white crystal substance inside.

He closed the case and said, "Get all this checked, will you, and listed. I suggest you let Drug Squad check the unlabelled bottles. Book it all into Crime property and at no time be alone with it. I do not want any allegations that we have planted something. I will ask you to count the money first so I can put someone's mind at rest about how much we have recovered. I'll follow you down in a few minutes, and please send another officer in here with me."

Saul sat down at Atkins's desk and found the contents rather interesting. Most of the documentation he found he seized as evidence. The woman, Margaret, came into the office and looked positively cheerful.

She smiled at him. "Are you looking for anything in particular? Maybe I can help you."

"Evidence."

"Then I know I can. He has a lock-up cupboard in the storeroom. He's been putting a lot of things in there recently and the only key is that yale one on the key ring there."

"Now, why would you be so willing to help us?"

"Because I loathe the man and his surly chum Potter. Mr Ted has made my life hell and all the other girls as well. He is spiteful, devious and very rude. We have lost quite a few good workers already because of him. If I didn't have two daughters to put through university, I'd have left ages ago. We all like Mr Atkins, and Mr William and most of the other auctioneers but Mr Ted is a very different kettle of fish. I have worked here since I left school and it was only when he came here that it stopped being a happy place."

"I see. Someone tipped us off about the plane ticket, and it looked like we were just in time. I would like to thank them and so, when he finds out, will Mr Atkins. I will be very grateful for any help you can give us."

"You just did thank me. I saw the ticket yesterday evening as he was packing up. I thought it looked like he was going to a bunk. I hoped if I rang your office, someone would come in time. I'm sorry I was a bit off when you arrived, but I worried you might fall for his arrogant assumption of total innocence. I am afraid I listened in on your conversation, I switched the intercom on. You are wonderful, thank you and that is from all of us. The day he is convicted, we will throw a party to which you and all your polite and tidy officers are invited; now, do you want tea or coffee?"

"Coffee, please, white, no sugar. Thank you. I only know you as Margaret. Would you be willing to sit down with one of my officers and give a statement?"

"Too right I would, especially if it is that handsome one called Toby. Shall I show you or him the cupboard?"

Saul smiled and called over to the police officers in the office outside the door. "PC Wilson, could you accompany this lady to a store cupboard and when your team have searched it, take a statement from her?"

PC Wilson smiled and said, "My pleasure, sir."

"Can you also find the auditor and ask him to come and see me?"

The auditor was a small man with thick spectacles. He said, "I was going to call you in any way. I am Peter Dearmer. Mr Atkins senior told me to expect you and to hand anything untoward over to you. Can I start by bringing you up to date with what I have found so far?"

"In brief, I take it we need to call in the Fraud Squad?"

"I am afraid so. There are altered documents and a huge amount of money missing. The computer files are encrypted and will take some decoding, but it looks like a huge case. We are talking millions, not thousands. I have a team of computer buffs working on that already. The files at the Skipton branch are the same and my colleague is there seizing everything; then, they will be checking the other branches. Mr Atkins senior told me to hand it over to you and if possible, try to keep the business going. Have you recovered any actual money because I have not found much here? It is rather strange, but it all seems to have been sent over to the Skipton office and taken out from there over at least a couple of months. I do know that most of the transactions have occurred late at night, but I thought the offices closed by eight p.m. at the latest."

"I know how that was done and you have confirmed a suspicion for me. What do you need from us now?"

"I would like to look in here if I may. Mr Ted wouldn't let us in here. He said it was all personal stuff in this office; he very rudely told us to go away and he would arrange another day for us to come here. when it was convenient to him."

"Yes, after he had done a bunk trip to Spain. May I leave you to confer with the officers I am sending to you? I need to go and book the charming Mr Ted Atkins into the police station. Here is my card. Please tell Mr Atkins senior what you have found as soon as you can. Can you also tell him that we found a great deal of cash in the briefcase that Mr Ted had?"

Half an hour later, Saul walked into the custody suite at the local police station.

The custody sergeant said, "I am so glad you are here, sir. Atkins is being utterly uncooperative. He has been seen by the police surgeon, who has given us tablets should he need them. Atkins will not tell us anything at all, not even his name, date of birth, address, or anything about himself. He is demanding everything, however. First, a solicitor from Skipton, so we rang them, and the solicitor said he could not and did not want to represent him as he was already acting for his father and brother. Nor will any other solicitor from that firm attend. They suggested a local firm here and someone is on their way. Atkins lost his temper when I told him, so I put him in cell to calm down. Can you please outline the reasons for his detention?"

Atkins was produced from his cell and given his rights. Saul said to him, "You are under arrest for fraud and false accounting and theft but also for assault occasioning actual bodily harm at Skipton auction mart on the sixteenth of the month and for violently resisting arrest today. You do not have to say anything, but it may harm your defence if you fail to mention anything now which you later rely on in court."

Atkins screamed, "Poppycock! You assaulted me! You came into MY office and attacked me. He is making the whole thing up; you only have his word about what happened in my office."

The sergeant smiled and said, "On the contrary, I have just watched and listened to the complete recording of what happened and that will be produced as evidence. Chief Superintendent Catchpole, like all the officers on such an investigation, caries a lapel mike and camera."

"That is entrapment; you mean you came into my personal office as trespassers with a secret camera."

Saul looked him in the face and said, "And it may interest you to know that we were invited into the premises by your father, who gave us permission to look anywhere we wished. The office you state is your office is part of the firm's holdings. It may also interest you to know that Mr Harold Potter has also been arrested and is being most cooperative. His house is also being searched."

"Well, I only have your word for that. You are just saying that to trick me. I demand to speak to Harold now!

You may have been fooled by my senile old father and my obnoxious brother, but I am not taken in by your lies. I refuse to have anything more to do with you. I demand to speak to the chief constable; get him here now. I know him quite well."

The sergeant said, "You really are not helping yourself, Mr Atkins. Mr Catchpole has been more than fair with you. You are not in a position to demand anything. When the solicitor arrives, you may consult with her and you will be given a chance to put your side of things in an interview, which will be recorded, as is everything that occurs here in the custody suite."

"Her? I'm not having a female solicitor."

"That is up to you. I suggest you calm down. When the solicitor arrives, you may consult with her or not, as you wish. The more you try to obstruct us, the longer it will take. Until then, this officer will put you back into your cell."

"I said, you idiot, that I wished to speak to the chief constable. Now! Don't try to palm me off with anyone else. I know him."

Saul smiled and said, "It may interest you to know that he is aware of this case and in fact, authorised me to apply for the warrants. Has already been in touch with your father. His specific instructions to me were that if you should demand to speak to him, to tell you that he will see you in court. He stated to me that he does not know you but thinks you might have met his predecessor, who retired last year."

An hour later, Saul spoke to Inspector Bickerstaff, who had been interviewing Potter.

"Good news, guvnor, we have a full confession, implicating Edward Atkins in the theft of money from the company over several months. He also admitted being at Skipton Mart on the day of the murders and said Mr Ted rang him in a panic when they saw all the police there, and they then met up in the car park of the Burger King down the road; Atkins then gave Potter some clothes to hide including a torn Jacket that I think is the one you had a piece of, yes, I have it. Potter said he knew about Ted getting in through the drains but also said he never tried as he is claustrophobic. He is, too. We have had to put him in an open area. He says he knows nothing about the murders, and I believe him."

"Is he implicated in the fraud?"

"Yes, and admits his part in it. He was also due to fly out to Spain today but on a different flight. We had a passport and found a huge sum of cash cleverly hidden in a suitcase. He also told us the plan was that they would fly to Brazil a couple of days later. Both of them already have bank accounts in Spain and have put a lot of money into them from the firm's accounts. He said they had done that to make the banks think they were going to invest in property there to start a subsidiary business. He also said he was scared to death of Ted and was going to split from him and branch off as soon as he could. He will testify for us if we can cut him a deal."

"I see. I will consider it. Contact all the necessary agencies for me and get the ball rolling. I suggest we seize his passport and bail him so long as he signs on at least once a day. Well done, Geoff."

"I will. Are you all right, Saul? I hear you had another scarp?"

"I'm fine. I won this one, which made me feel much better. I'm not made of bone china, you know!"

"We know, we just worry about you."

"How touching, why?"

"If anything happened to you, we'd have to work under someone else and they might not be so kind."

"Rubbish! It would probably do you good. You wouldn't miss me after a month and my successor might be a lot kinder than I am."

"I doubt it."

"This is irrelevant as I am not leaving."

"Talking of leaving, Caroline asked me to put her on late as she says she is feeling sick in the mornings."

"Morning sickness? We knew this would happen sooner or later so do it. We need to bring her inside. Could she take on some of Fred's duties?"

"Yes, I considered that. He is going through a bad patch and agrees we will have to drastically cut his hours. I thought I should clear it with you, as Alan says he cannot make the decision as he is personally involved."

"Quite right, he would; you do know that when I retire, I think he will take over."

"I hope so; he is developing into Catchpole Mark two."

"Poor chap! Geoff, you know I am off tomorrow."

"Yes, Alan is covering. Family do, anything nice?"

"Nice, no; family, yes. My family, not Anna's. My nephew is speaking at the synagogue here, so I have to go."

"Well, I hope it goes well."

"So do I."

Ted Atkins refused to say anything when he was interviewed and refused to speak to the lady solicitor. Another solicitor was contacted and spoke briefly to him on the phone and arranged to attend later. Saul, having left everything being dealt with by his team, drove out to see Mr Atkins senior. He was a little surprised to find Mr William there as well.

He was invited in, and they sat in the elegant drawing room. "Mr Atkins, I am so sorry. It must be a terrible shock for you; You must feel so betrayed."

"Don't be sorry. If it had not been for your prompt action, I think we would be much worse off. I gather you got them before they fled to Spain. Will and I were just discussing it. Tell me, how did you know?"

"I had a tip-off. Someone on your staff was suspicious and has been for a long time. The staff have been most helpful to us; they are loyal to you and want to help getting things back as they should be."

"Why did they not tell me before?"

"Because if he had caught them out, they would have been sacked at the very least. I do want to tell you we have recovered in excess of two million pounds, and there is more in bank accounts that have now been frozen until the courts can return it to you. My officers are still counting a huge stash of money found at Mr Ted's house."

"Thank you, that is a great relief. The auditor told me it was him who attacked you that day."

"Yes, he admitted that."

"So, you think he is the killer?"

"No, Mr William, I don't. I cannot rule him out, but I don't believe that. We will have to see what transpires. He had no motive to kill those men that I know of. Time will tell."

"Not Eric, no, but he might have had with Herbert."

"Please, explain."

"Herbert Yorke was there the day my sister died. He was a young man then, a couple of years older than me. I know he helped in the search for them. I have been thinking about it. Herbert has always avoided Ted; he's always been polite, but I remember whenever Ted was around with me, he would be there, almost watching us. Ted and I had a real bust-up one day. I wouldn't give him something he wanted; I cannot even remember what it was. Afterwards, Herbert took me aside and told me to be careful of Ted and that he could be nasty. I do remember Ted sulked for days and later in the week, he deliberately slammed a door on my hand. He said it was an accident, of course, but I had two broken fingers, but I knew it was no accident."

"So why kill Herbert now?"

"I think Herbert knew something, found something out."

"Something about what Ted was doing?"

"I expect so."

"Did Ted have anything to do with Eric Rees?"

"He knew him; Eric drove to Hawes as well. I can't see they would have anything in common."

"How about Colin Boothby?"

"I can't see that either."

"Mr Catchpole, I know Ted is my son, but I will help you in any way I can. This is the final straw in our obviously failed attempts to help him. Would it help if I try and talk to him?"

"Well, he's not talking to anyone else at the moment. If he will talk to you and you can talk some sense into him, it might help him as well as us. I will ask them to tell him you would like to talk to him."

Will said, "How is young Colin? Has he said anything yet?"

"Not yet; he is improving and off the danger list; my next port of call is to his father."

"Then please tell James that we are desperately upset and will do anything to help if he needs us. Mr Catchpole, I need to tell you that as a family, we will ensure Ted has a good solicitor and legal help, but we are otherwise not wanting anything to do with him after all this is over."

"He is a very lucky man then. I am afraid he will need good legal help; he has dug himself into a very deep hole indeed. What I would find hard to forgive is his blatant betrayal of his family and of your family business. I am sorry to be the bearer of such tidings."

Chapter 9

When Saul got home that evening, his brother Abraham and his nephew Malachi were there. The atmosphere was a little strained and very polite. Anna had prepared a wonderful meal, which they ate in traditional Jewish style. After the meal, they adjourned to the lounge and sat down.

Saul asked, "So, how is the tailoring business doing, Abe?"

Abe replied, "Things could be better, but they could be worse. The cost of good quality cloth is rocketing, and thread is expensive now. We have to charge more, but there are more rich young men in the city who have made the business reasonably profitable. Not as good as I would like but young Ariel is coming on well. He is a very good tailor and goes to college one day a week and it will not be that long before I can make him a junior partner."

"Uncle Saul, what father is not saying is that business could be better, but things are not as they should be at home. Of course, I don't live there any more. I have my own flat, but my brothers are proving quite a disappointment."

"Is Ariel still living at home then, Abe?"

Once again, Malachi interjected, "Yes, but not for long. He is courting a good Jewish girl and they will be married very soon. I, of course, will be performing the ceremony. They will then move into the flat above the shop. Ariel knows his duties, unlike his brother Isaac, who is so like Uncle Jacob as to almost be a clone."

Saul tried again, "So, Abe, how is your health these days?"

"Father spends too much time in the business. He should be at home, resting more. I have told him I will happily do what I can to help him, on the administration side, of course. He sometimes says he is too tired to come to worship. He had a heart problem not long ago and should not have to tolerate Isaac's behaviour."

Saul drew in a long breath and looked at Malachi. "Tell me, Malachi, do you teach in the synagogue about the respect due to one's elders? How come you show so little to your father? I expect you to wish to prepare for tomorrow, don't you? Jake and I are very keen to hear you speak. As you know, we will both be there and in fact, he and his wife will be staying here afterwards. I gather you have not yet met his wife, Diana; I'm sure you are looking forward to it."

Malachi stormed out of the room and could be heard stomping up the stairs.

Abraham looked very relieved. "I apologise for his behaviour, Saul. He is trying to take over my life and everything I have anything to do with. As he said, I did have a bit of a heart scare, but it is sorted now. I wanted your advice about young Isaac."

"I thought you disapproved of me?"

"Not at all. You have never denied your roots, even if you do not advertise them. Isaac is causing problems at home. He has left school where he did very well and is due to start college soon, but he cannot seem to make up his mind what he wants to do. He is certainly not interested in the business; that is clear, and he and Mal are constantly fighting. He will not accept Mal's guidance over anything, and although Esther and I have tried, he said he does not wish to go to the synagogue and he wants out. He has asked several times to move away. He is sixteen but although he is honest, he cannot be on his own yet."

"What is it he wants to do?"

"Follow you into the police."

"And you don't want that?"

"I wouldn't mind. You have done very well made the senior ranks and have respect, honour even."

"I thought you were ashamed of me and Jake?"

"Far from it with you. Jake, he is another matter. What is this wife of his like? I take it she isn't one of us?"

"Diana is a remarkable and very strong woman. He has become quite respectable since they got together. We love her."

"Jake is Jake, always fun but no respect for any form of authority. Seeing Isaac's unhappiness has made me look at things a little differently. Maybe we were too hard on Jake, which is why I want to see him and tell him that and ask his forgiveness."

"Abe, are you ill?"

"No, Saul, I am not. I think I have just woken up to the real world. As I said, I had a bit of a scare a few months back, but I love my family. Life is too short to hold grudges. It isn't for me to dictate how my brothers or even my children live. That must be their choice. It has taken me long enough to see it."

"All right, now how is my niece, Rachel?"

"She is doing fine, and she wants to come into the business and is studying hard for S levels. She is a talented designer."

"Do you really want me to talk to Isaac?"

"Yes, I do. He really respects you but thinks I am an old fuddy-duddy. He does not know Jake and I do think they should meet."

Malachi, who had obviously been listening just the other side of the open door, strutted in, "Father, Jake could corrupt him. Just because Isaac is being difficult does not mean you have to accept his behaviour."

"Well, at the moment, this is not going to happen. He and your mother barely speak, and I am at my wits' end what to do, which is why I am asking the advice of my elder brother."

Anna, who had been sitting quietly knitting and listening with growing annoyance, put down her knitting and said, "Saul dear, could you help me with something in the kitchen?"

Saul followed her into the kitchen, where Anna firmly shut the door. They were gone some time and then returned, and Saul said to Abraham, "Would it help if Isaac came and stayed with us for a while?"

Abe looked up with relief, he smiled and said, "I am sure Anna has enough to do; we can't ask that of you."

Anna sat down beside him and said, "Actually, Abraham, I suggested it. He can go to college here. We have the space and with the girls away at boarding school, he can settle down and make his own decisions. If he wants to go to the synagogue, Saul will take him."

"You would do that for my son after the way we have treated you?"

"No, I would do it for Saul. I know you do not approve of me, but I am not a bad person."

"Anna, that is most generous of you, and Saul is a lucky chap to have you. For ages, I couldn't see beyond the fact that you are not Jewish, but now I think I am learning wisdom. You are a good wife and mother that I do know."

Malachi stood in front of his father, "Father, I think we should find somewhere for Isaac where he will be encouraged to follow our faith, a proper Jewish home, not here."

"I know you do, Malachi but you are not the head of the family. Actually, Saul is."

"Well, I don't think he should have anything to do with Uncle Jacob, who might make him worse."

Saul said, "We see a lot of Jake. It will not harm Isaac to get to know him; he won't try to influence him; he's always been his own man."

"Yes, to move in dubious circles and deny our faith! Like you have."

"Malachi, I respect your faith and your devotion to it. Jake and I have chosen our ways. Let Isaac do the same."

"Uncle Saul, have you no sense of obligation to your own people? Do you want us persecuted and despised?"

"I respect my tradition, yes, but I am what I am. I do not wish to have a lecture on the Holocaust and the history of the Jewish nation here in this house. You have made it plain how you feel and your expectations of your own family but you can lecture them all you like when you actually have a family of your own. Here, everyone is free to make their own choices; Isaac is welcome here."

Malachi was obviously furious and stood face to face with Saul, who was quite bit taller than him.

"You are wrong; if you will not listen to those wiser than yourself, I will go to my room and prepare for tomorrow when you might just learn that I am wiser than you."

There was a stunned silence for a few minutes as he stormed up the stairs and they could hear his bedroom door slam.

Abraham looked at Anna and said, "I am so, so sorry. How could he be so rude? He is more than half the trouble with Isaac; he will not let up on the boy, who is desperately trying to be his own man. It is not unnatural for him to rebel; you did Saul and so did Jake. I was never strong enough. Saul, there's a question that Isaac asked me that I do not know the answer to. It seems to be important to him to know and I thought you might have the answer."

"What is it then?"

"You, Jake and Isaac all have red hair and blue eyes. Not a very Jewish trait. Mother had black hair and grey eyes, and father had brown hair and hazel eyes. Mal rather spitefully suggested that Isaac was not my son. Do you know?"

"Yes, I asked that question too. No, not that my mother cheated but where it comes from. You never met mother's mother, did you?"

"No, she died when I was very little."

"I just remember her, but then she had white hair. She had brilliant blue eyes I was told she used to dye her hair black. She was not born a Jew, you know; she was a convert. I met her sister once, who had red hair and freckles."

"Why was I never told?"

"Did you ask?"

"No, it never occurred to me until Isaac brought it up because of something Mal said to him. Would you really have Isaac to stay?"

"Yes, we discussed it. Anna suggested that when he sees the hours I put in, he might just go off the idea of joining the police. When do you want to bring him up here?"

"As soon as I can. There is not a good atmosphere at home and Esther is most stressed by the whole thing, and so am I. Why did Jake agree to come to the synagogue tomorrow?"

"I'm not sure. Be warned, he may well try to take Mal down a peg or two, which I think is long overdue. Abe, how could you let him become such a pompous, arrogant bully?"

"I don't know. He is very controlling; He feels that now he is the youngest rabbi, he should dictate to my family and everyone else. He is so sanctimonious as to be offensive sometimes; that is why I suggested it was time he had his own place for which he expects me to pay, by the way. He likes to sit as the head of the family and only grudgingly makes way for me. He is treating me like a weak-minded old fool to be preached at. He has done well, yes, but he thinks he has all the answers. I think I have only just woken up to how nasty he is."

"I am sure Jake will put him right then. He has always been the cleverer one of the family and as for Diana, she has more brains than the lot of us put together. I am sure you will like her; we do."

"Is Jake happy at last?"

"Deliriously so. He has changed a lot. He worships her."

"Does she work?"

"Yes, she is a civil servant, very high up. I'm not sure exactly what she does but she works mainly from home."

"How odd, I didn't think they did that."

"Well, she does. She is some sort of consultant, instructor."

"I must ask her about it."

"By all means. If you want to get to know her, talk about orchids, dog farming or wine. She is a fascinating woman."

Later, when Anna and Saul were in bed, Anna said, "He won't leave it, Saul. He will try to find out exactly what she does. I wonder what she will tell him."

"So do I! Are you sure about Isaac coming here? He could be a lot of trouble."

"Quite sure. Once he is out of Mal's way, I expect he will calm down. Mal is warped, a fanatic you do know that?"

"Yes. And pompous and arrogant. Poor Abe. He was so proud of him and now is being treated like a child. Are you sure you won't come and hear Mal speak tomorrow?"

"Quite sure. Diana and I are going to prepare a suitable meal. I asked the girls if they wanted to come home this weekend and they very firmly said not. I also asked both the boys, who gave the same answer. They all like Abe and even Esther but want nothing to do with Malachi."

"Their choice. I was hoping to ask Diana to help me think something through, to do with this latest case. I would be grateful for your input as well."

"What's wrong?"

"It is like there are several different things going on, all apparently unconnected but they have all come together at the same time and place. It is like a ball of wool that the dogs have been playing with. It needs unravelling. Did the dogs growl at Mal?"

"Yes, and slunk off to their beds. They like Abe but will not go near Mal."

"I like those dogs; they have taste."

The next day, after Saul, Jake and Abraham had returned from the synagogue, they came into the kitchen where Di and Anna were laughing. Jake looked amazingly innocent, and Di paused, looked at him and then said, "Where is your nephew? Jake, what have you done?"

"He's coming later. He said he needed to speak to another group there. I don't think he liked some of my questions."

"Oh, Jake, did you have to make life difficult?"

"Yes, I did. Abe, how could you let him become so big-headed?"

"I don't know. He really came over as a fanatic, didn't he? I just hope he can wind his neck in when he gets back here, where I can really tell him what I think. Saul, you could have backed me up a bit more at the synagogue."

"Jake, I am simply not in your league. Abraham, may I introduce you to my sister-in-law, Diana. For simplicity's sake, we call her Di and my wife Anna. Di, meet my younger brother."

"I am so pleased to meet you, Abraham. Jake has told me all about you. Can I get you a drink?"

"Thank you, yes; if my son and Jake are going to have a religious debate, I think I am going to need one. We could be in for a major row. I hope not."

"Well, I intend to keep out of it. My theological knowledge is not that good. I leave the academic things to Jake. Now, tell me about the rest of your family; I understand Isaac is coming to stay here?"

Di and Abraham were soon chatting happily out in the garden. Anna said to Saul, "OK, what happened?"

"Nothing much. He spoke well but was totally inflexible. Without any humour or any form of compromise. He came over as, 'I say this, I am right and everyone else is wrong. He asked for questions, silly boy, hoping, no doubt, to impress us with more pearls of wisdom, but Jake had some detailed argument that the chief Rabbi had used recently. How did you know about that, Jake?"

"If you must know, I looked up on the net. I rang our local rabbi and found out what Mal was going to speak on and did some research. I am sorry, Anna but he could be quite insufferable later."

"Well, I am keeping out of it. What is Abe talking to Diana about?"

"I'll give you two guesses. She seems to be making him laugh. You know he is becoming human again, Jake, more so than I remember in a long time."

"No, you are wrong there. When you were the serious grammar school prefect, he and I spent a lot of time together; We ganged upon you often."

"Oh, I remember all right. At the time, you accused me of being pompous. You were both very naughty sometimes."

"Of course, we were. It was our job as younger brothers!"

"Yes, and you got me into some right scrapes; I remember several where I had to think quickly to get you out of them. Then you two grew up a bit and we became a good trio."

"Yes, they were good times. Do you remember when we borrowed that boat to get across the river?"

"Yes, I do. We nearly got caught. I put it back while you two went to the fun fair with my pocket money. Which you still owe me for, by the way."

"A fiver, wasn't it?"

"It was. I wouldn't have minded but at the time, you two were grounded, so I was the one who got in trouble because you were not supposed to be out."

Jake put his hand in his pocket and handed Saul five five-pound notes.

"Here you are. We never did pay you back; I ate so much sweet stuff I was sick and so was Abe."

"Don't be daft; put your money away!"

"No, I insist! I'll get half back from Abe."

Anna laughed and said, "Do tell me more, Jake; this is fascinating."

She and Jake went back into the kitchen and Saul joined the others in the garden. Abe was laughing, "Saul, you said she was knowledgeable, and she is. She has told me a very plausible tale and I don't believe a word of it; Jake is a lucky chap."

"Yes, I know; come on inside and distract Jake from telling my wife all my dreadful boyhood adventures."

"That sounds good. Maybe I can remember some. All right, so long as Mal is not there. He would disapprove most strongly. He always was a pious little weasel. I have only just seen how bad he has become, the little toad!"

"Tell me, Abe, do all the family liken those they don't like to animals?"

"Oh, we got it all from Saul. Did you know he spent hours at the zoo and even won a biology prize? Mind you, he also won a maths prize and loads for art. He was head boy, too. We gave him hell over it."

"I remember only too well."

"Yes. He played hockey for the school and rugby but not for long. He wasn't heavy enough; he did long distance running. Jake did rugby. He was plenty big enough. I was always a little weed. I had asthma as a kid, so I wasn't sporty."

"You were good at lots of other things, Abe. He was in the school play every year."

"You played Shylock in *The Merchant of Venice*. He was brilliant, Di, he really was."

"No, I wasn't; I was racked with stage fright and very mediocre!"

"I remember it well. I was in the crowd scene. He became this nasty, grasping man and had everyone spellbound. It got a great write-up; I've still got it somewhere."

"I knew this reminiscing was a bad idea."

The five of them had a very happy hour, chatting and laughing together until Malachi was dropped off by the local rabbi, who declined an invitation to stay for a meal and left.

The meal was eaten in almost total silence, and afterwards, they all adjourned to the sitting room. Jake and Mal started debating something, at which Anna and Di retreated to the kitchen, where they watched a film, trying to drown out the raised voices from the other room.

The doorbell went and Anna opened it to find a man in an impeccable black suit and black tie who said, "I am so sorry to hear your bad news; I am the undertaker you called. I believe Mr Catchpole has passed away?"

"I don't think so; we have four of them loudly debating theology in the lounge right now. No, no one has died. Who called you?"

"A Mrs Diana Catchpole."

"Well, that is both of us. Come in a minute, I think I know what has happened. I'll fetch my husband. Which Mr Catchpole was it?"

"A Mr Saul Catchpole. You mean this is a nasty hoax?"

"Yes, I am afraid so. I expect it is my sister who is mentally ill. She likes to cause upset."

Saul managed to reassure the man, thanked him for his time and when he had left rang the hospital in which Ruth was supposed to be.

He then said, "Ruth has got out again! Standby to repel borders. This is all I need. Look, could you two stop World War Three in the sitting room? Abe and I opted out ages ago. We only stayed to prevent violence."

Diana went into the sitting room and found Abe sitting nervously by the door. Malachi was red in the face and looking furious, and Jake was sitting with an annoying smile in his face.

"Enough, both of you! From this point on, there will be no more religious discussion; I'm bored with it, even if you two are not. The rest of us certainly are. I am surprised at you, Malachi, causing dissent in your uncle's house, especially on your sabbath day. Jake, behave yourself or go out in the garden or something. Should you ever come to my house, young man, you will show respect to your elders. Jake, stop winding him up."

"What would you know about our faith?"

Jake winced and so did Saul, who was standing behind Diana.

"A lot more than you think; I spent six months in a kibbutz in Israel. Don't make assumptions about people, Malachi. It is both dangerous and foolish. It is not your place to preach to those whom you should respect. Any true rabbi would know that. Abraham, please could you come with me? Saul may need your help. We have an impending crisis and these two will not be any help, but you might be. You two stay away from each other and pray for wisdom and guidance because you both need it."

Malachi began to protest, but Diana and Abraham walked into another room. Jake went and collected the dogs and took them out for a walk, leaving Malachi shouting at himself.

Abe followed Diana into the conservatory and looked at her with respect.

"That needed saying, thank you. I was told you are a strong woman, something I respect greatly. You are obviously used to command. I am so sorry it got out of hand."

"Well, it would; one stubborn, unconventional man and a zealot with a high opinion of himself were never going to get on. Why ever did you let him become so arrogant?"

"You're right, he is. I suppose I just put it down to devotion, but he has gone way too far. He has no respect for me, certainly. He thinks he is Jehovah's new prophet

136

and won't let anyone tell him he is wrong. What should I do?"

"That is up to you. If he were a Christian, I would suggest he became a monk and learnt some humility. I am sure there is something similar in Judaism. He will wreck your family if you let him. No wonder Isaac is rebelling."

"And it's my fault. You are a wise woman, Diana; now, what is this crisis, and how can I help?"

Saul then spoke to Abraham in the kitchen and Diana went back into the sitting room to fetch her bag. Malachi glowered at her almost shouted, "You have no right to speak to me like that; I shall tell my uncle that you have to leave this house, or I will. My father and will leave if you stay."

"You foolish young man! Please tell Saul that and see what he says and your father, who no doubt has supported you and maintained you all these years while you studied, without a word of protest. How old are you, twenty-eight, thirty? Apart from religious bigotry, exactly what have you contributed to your home, financially, I mean?"

"God's work needs no payment."

"No, but food and warmth and clothes do. Who provided them?"

"My parents were honoured to help me."

"Really? Have you ever had a proper job? How long are you going to leech off them? It is time for you to grow up."

"How dare you? It's none of your business."

"Maybe not. They care too much to say it; someone needs to tell you to burst your self-inflated bubble of pomposity. I admit my husband is partly to blame, but he is an opinion backed by a lifetime of reading, experience and knowledge, none of which you seem to have. Wind your neck in, boy, before someone chops your head off. The mere fact that you have got as far as you have does not make you perfect; it means you have a lot more to learn."

"Well, I wouldn't expect anything but abuse from a gentile like you."

"I don't remember saying what my religious ties were. I warn you, do not make assumptions. If I wish to worship tadpoles, it would be none of your business."

"No Jewish woman would talk to a rabbi like that."

"To me, you are no rabbi. You are just a spoiled brat. Your mother may revere you, but I know many Jewish women who discipline their children and guide them and always will."

Diana picked up her bag and calmly left the room. As she did so, Abraham pulled her into the study next door.

"I'm sorry, I eavesdropped. Why could I not see that? You we were quite right; we have paid for everything. He has never contributed a penny. I have no intention of leaving because he has been told to behave himself unless Saul throws me out. I'd like to stay for a day or two. Mal can find his own way home. I think I need to ring Esther."

"Saul and Jake both love you, Abe, I know that. Otherwise, why would they take on Isaac? I rather like you, too, and you are very much their brother. I am sorry I was so rude to your boy, but someone had to say it."

"I know, and it should have been me, but I don't have your command of the language. Can you tell Saul what was said?"

"I think he heard it himself; yes, he is just up the stairs here."

Minutes later, Malachi came down the stairs with his case and ordered his father to leave with him. When Saul refused to tell Jake and Di to leave, Abe said in a cold and calm voice, "No, son, I am still welcome here and intend to stay. Find your own way home to your flat, not my house."

"Then give me the car keys."

"No, that is my car, and it is staying here. Use public transport."

"You have to take me home!"

"No, I don't. Saul, can he get home by public transport from here?"

"Easily. The forty-seven bus goes from the bottom of the road directly to the main railway station. It should be due in about fifteen minutes. From there, he can catch a train direct to Kings Cross. It takes about two and a half hours."

"You can't expect me to use a bus or a train!"

"Why not?"

"I am a rabbi. I don't travel like that."

"Then learn. rabbi or not. Us ordinary mortals have to use busses, so can you."

"Father, give me the fare then!"

"No, you have money, use that."

"I don't have enough."

"I am sure there is a cash point at the station; you could, of course, apologise to everyone here if you need their help."

"I'd rather walk. I didn't bring my bank card with me; I'll have to find someone at the synagogue."

Malachi stormed off down the drive and Anna followed him, catching up with him by the bus stop.

She sat on the bench beside him and said, "You rather brought that upon yourself, you know; I know you lost your temper, which really didn't help, and I recognise it as a family trait. Do you really not have enough?"

"I've about ten pounds on me."

"Then I will lend you enough to get home, but I want it repaid on your word of honour."

"You have it. I am sorry but they don't understand."

"When you have calmed down and can look at it in an adult manner, I think you will understand why they were cross. Here is £100, which should be sufficient to get you home. Please try not to upset anyone else today?"

They waited until the bus arrived and she saw him safely on to it. She walked slowly back to the house and met Jake coming in with the dogs from walk.

"Has he gone?"

"Yes. Jake, how could you provoke that?"

"I didn't, he did. I tried to debate with him, but his arguments had holes you could fly a jumbo through. Then he got personal and insulted Abe, Saul, me and then you and, more dangerously, Diana. I just hope she didn't hear what he said. Then he started on his mother, and that made me see red. Poor Abe, to think he suddenly saw his precious eldest son for what he really was: a twisted, sly little creep. I also became aware that Abe was actually frightened of him. I am sorry, Anna; I apologise to you and Saul and will leave if you want me to. I just needed to calm down. I'll ring Abe to apologise to him."

"He's still here. He agrees with you; I got the impression that having his brothers there and some backup gave him strength. I think the angriest one is Di and yes, she did hear everything."

"Oh dear, I am in trouble then; I am so sorry and, in your house, too,"

"Apology accepted. Religion is a topic banned for the day. Now Ruth is on her way here; we think she has escaped. That is all we need!"

"Poor Saul, poor you. I could do with someone to fight right now. I'll sort her out,"

"You will do no such thing. Di has a cunning plan if Ruth comes. We need you out of the way, me too. It looks like we are taking the dogs for another tour of the park, and we must keep out of sight. Saul has moved our car and his."

When they walked back into the house minutes later, Jake made a full apology to Saul and then to Abraham. Saul smiled and said, "It is over. Have you faced Di yet?"

"Not yet. Where is she?"

"I think she is upstairs, but leave it; she is working it out how to repel Ruth if she turns up. Now, we were discussing Isaac and what he wants to do. Abe is arranging for him to come up here by train tomorrow. He will spend a bit of time with him here and we would like you to, as well. You might help by showing him that being independent can help."

Abraham smiled at Jake and then hugged him. "I don't blame you for saying what you did. My eyes have been opened to Mal, and I don't like what I see much. I have rung Esther and told her and was shocked at what she told me. She said she has seen it and is terrified of him. He has been behaving in an appalling manner when I am not there. She also told me how he treats his siblings as well. I put it all on speaker so Saul heard too. Ariel has, to some extent, held his own, but Rachel and Isaac are terrified of Mal. She doesn't want him back in the house, nor do I, now my eyes have been opened to what he is. I will ask for your help and advice."

"Then together, I am sure we can come up with something; Saul, is Ruth really out again?"

"Yes. I despair of that hospital. Their security is hopeless. She put on a doctor's coat and just strolled out. They didn't even know until I called them and then found it on their security cameras."

"Is she not in a secure unit?"

"Allegedly. It was during a staff tea break. She is now circulated as wanted; as soon as she shows up, we must ring for backup."

"So that was why the undertaker came; that was spiteful."

"Abe, so is she. I wonder what else she has done."

Diana walked into the room and looked at Jake. "Exactly what did you tell Malachi about my religious beliefs?"

"Not much, I said I didn't really know, from which he assumed you didn't really have any. I did tell him you were very tolerant and broadminded about such things."

"No, Jake, I think you said more than that; you said if he believed God was a tadpole and he worshipped him as such, I'd probably accept it and wouldn't want any other beliefs imposed on me. Is that not, right? Abe?"

"Er, yes, I think something like that."

"Yes, well, maybe I did. Di, are you still talking to me? I am so, so sorry."

"Good. I said some pretty harsh things to him; I am sorry, Abe but he needed to hear it from someone."

"Don't be. As a matter of fact, Diana, what are your religious beliefs?"

"I'm not sure I have any. I have not yet met a religion that I can wholly believe in or accept. There is good in most of them but not that match how I feel. Agnostic, I suppose."

"So, I cannot convert you?"

"No. Does anyone want a drink because? I certainly do. Hang on, I think I hear Ruth approaching. Places everyone. Anna, you and Jake go out the back gate with the dogs. Saul, you go upstairs and ring for backup. Abe, come with me. Do as we discussed and follow my lead."

A few minutes later Diana answered the front door to find Ruth standing there. She asked, "Yes, can I help you?"

"I want to see Diana Catchpole; she is my sister."

"I am so sorry, but I am afraid they moved out yesterday. I was so sorry when I heard he had died. The undertaker must have the wrong address. My husband and

I were so lucky to find a fully furnished house so quickly to rent. Can I give you the agent's details? I am sure they can put you in touch; I think they said it was Wakefield they were going to. We only arrived two days ago from South Africa and are house-hunting in the area. Alan and I were both teaching out there, in Soweto."

"You're a teacher, so am I. Is your husband in?"

"Yes, oh, here he is. Alan, this lady is Mrs Catchpole's sister; she's a teacher too. Do you have the number for the letting agency?"

"Yes, I'll look, ah, here it is, give them a ring; the Catchpoles were going to find a smaller house, I believe. Please tell me he isn't dead, is he?"

"No, he's not dead; it must have been a mix-up. Thanks for your help. If they do contact you, could you tell her I called her, not him? He and I don't get on."

"Of course, we will. Who shall I say called?"

"Just say Ruth. Sorry to bother you."

They watched as Ruth walked back down the driveway and into the street, where she was met by a police car, put inside it and driven away.

Abe smiled and said, "That worked well; how simple, but how clever."

"It will only work once, though; now, let's get that drink."

Chapter 10

The next morning, Saul spent some time catching up on the progress made with the cases. Geoff Bickerstaff came into the office and said, "Colin Boothby seems much better and has started talking. He wants to tell you what he remembers. It is almost as though he has woken up from a dream. Do you want to come?"

"I do. We had better record everything. Has Ted Atkins said anything more?"

"Yes, lots, mainly about how he took the money that he insists is all his and he hasn't actually stolen anything. He denies knowing anything about the murders. He really is the most arrogant, insufferable man and so rude with it."

"Believe me, he is not even in the same league as me and my eldest nephew. Do you believe him about the murders?"

"Yes, and no. He knows something, probably who it was but will not say."

"How much money was in his briefcase?"

"Just over £250,000. He initially did not want to speak to his father but has changed his mind and will see him this afternoon. Oh, and we have picked up Pickstaff in the red-light area of Bradford."

"Has he said anything?"

"Not yet. He was too drunk and has had to sleep it off."

"A day full of interviews then."

"Looks like it; how did your family day go?"

"Not all bad; one of my nephews is coming to stay with us for a while. His name is Isaac, he's sixteen and wants to be a policeman."

"Good for him."

Colin Boothby looked much better. His head was still swathed in bandages, but he had colour back in his cheeks. His father was sitting beside his bed when Saul and Geoff came in.

"Do you mind my being here?"

"Not at all, Mr Boothby, if Colin wants you here."

"Sir, I have nothing to hide. I didn't kill anyone, honest. I didn't even know anyone had been killed until Dad told me."

"I accept that. Now, can you tell us what you can remember? I'll record it if you don't mind. Take your time and we can stop if you need a break."

"OK. It all began when I met this girl, Alison Pickstaff. I loved her a lot. She was a grand Yorkshire Lass. I went out with her when she had split up from seeing my neighbour's son. It was only when I heard they had split up that I asked her out. He and I had words about it, but we made it up later. Mr Goodyard's son, it was. Anyway, Alison's dad hates me. He tried to stop me seeing her. He had done the same with Mr Goodyard's lad. Old man Pickstaff was horrid to Alison sometimes; she told me he locked her in the house, and I knew she was terrified of him. We used to meet secretly whenever we could. Her dad even threatened me and my dad, too. Alison and I would meet at the end of their road, and I'd take her for a coffee or a bit of a walk. She could never stop long 'cos he was always checking up on her."

"Was he violent?"

"She said yes, he was. He found me with her once and tried to beat up on me, but I hit him back and blacked his eye. He's a right fat bugger, not fit at all. He was a right bully and like all bullies, he never took me on again. Dad said she and I could live at our farm, and we were planning to get married. Her dad went off on some railway jaunt. He is crackers about trains, anything to do with the railway. Then, when he came back, Alison said there was a big problem, and I wouldn't want her no more and she would have to call it off. I went round to see her, but he wouldn't let me in or her out to talk to me. I rang her later and she was really upset. She said things were dreadful and my going round would make them worse. I didn't hear from her for three days and then I was told she had died, real sudden like. I went round to see if it was true, but he wouldn't answer the door, but I knew he was in. His car was there."

"So, what did you do?"

"I asked around and found a doctor had been there. Not the local one; I'd never heard of this doctor before. I rang this doctor up and he said it was this virus thing and it was very sudden, and he said he was very sorry. I was gutted but I found out about the funeral and went to it. The only flowers on her coffin were the ones I had given the undertaker for her. He was there and glared at me and said he would send back the ring I had given her. He did too, in the post in a brown envelope, second class."

"Did he give you any explanation?"

"He wouldn't speak to me at all."

"Then what?"

"Well, I felt lost for ages. Sometimes, I took flowers to the grave. I will never stop loving her. It took ages for me to get my head around it. I went round to her house again, but he had moved. I got his new address from the new people there but there wasn't much I could do."

"So, what changed?"

"I was putting something on the computer for Dad and I went on the net. I realised I could find out about this virus thing, and I did, and it did seem to fit what this doctor had said. I sort of accepted it then, but I was watching the box at my mate's house one night and they had this doctor on the news, something about a medical council and he had got some'at wrong and had been struck off. It was only then I wondered if he had got Alison's death wrong. I decided I needed to talk to her father ask a few questions."

"And did you talk to him?"

"Not at first; I wrote to him and asked him to contact me. I got no reply, twice, so I went up to Carlisle and waited for him where he works at the railway station there. He was not pleased to see me and told me to leave him alone. I said I would go on meeting him there until he did talk to me, so he agreed and said he would meet me at the graveyard and talk to me there. He said he wanted to talk to me alone."

"When was this?"

"Well, I knew I would be going to the auction mart that day and I said I would meet him from there, so I brought some roses and walked down and waited there. He was late but he eventually turned up. He tried to kick the flowers off the grave, but I stopped him. I said I was going to the coppers because I didn't believe this virus thing and even then, I thought it was the doctor who got it wrong. He got really angry, and we had a bit of a scuffle and I said if that was how he felt, he could talk to you lot. I walked back to the mart and was going to ring the police from there. I also needed to get my facts right and wanted somewhere quiet. Norman said the cattle ring was not being used, so I went there and sat down and got my phone out. The next thing I can remember was being very cold and wet, and there were sheep all around me. I think I was in some sort of animal trailer; I must have passed out again because the next thing I knew was this really bad headache and I was lying in some gorse bushes; it was like a dream, a really bad one. I was covered in blood and in sheep shit. I knew I was high up, like on a moor, but I didn't know where, and it was dark."

"Did you see anyone around?"

"No one. I started walking down this small road. I tell you; I was that scared; I was almost wetting myself. I couldn't walk properly either. Then there was this house with a light on, and I sort of thought I had been there before, but this man came out. I hid. I thought I knew him but couldn't remember how or why. He went back, so I followed a track and then I knew I had been there before;

I couldn't remember why, but I found a cave, a big one, so I sheltered in it from the wind. My headache was that bad I thought I was dying. I tried to lie down, but it hurt more, so I just sat leaning against this rock. I think I must have gone to sleep 'cos the next thing I knew, it was light and these people came and put me on a quad and took me back to a warm place. I couldn't even see properly by then. Then I think they sat me in a car and the next thing I remember, I was feeling better and warmer, and I woke up here in the hospital."

"Have you been told how you got here?"

"Yes, Dad said you saw me, but I don't remember that at all."

"Has he told you about Alison?"

"Yes, he said you dug her up. What did you find out?"

"She did not die from a virus; she was injected with a poison."

"I knew it! I reckon he did her in because she wanted to come away and marry me."

"Did you know she was pregnant?"

"She can't have been, well, not by me anyway. We decided to wait, you see, do it properly after we got married. That was the way she wanted it to be."

"Was she seeing anyone else?"

"No way. I know she wasn't. Was that the problem? Oh God! I'll bet it was her father. She used to say he was horrible to her, but if I asked why, she'd cry and I didn't want to hurt her more."

"Well, we will soon know because we have taken DNA samples. Her father has been arrested on suspicion of her murder."

"Good, he made her life hell. Are you going to arrest me too?"

"No, because we believe you."

"What has been done with her body?"

"It has been reburied by the vicar and put back into her grave; It was very dignified."

"So long as I can put flowers on it."

"When it happened, I was there. I put a bunch of white roses on her grave because I knew that was what you would have wanted. I hope you don't mind?"

"Thanks. I didn't know policemen cared that much; that was kind of you."

"Yes, Mr Catchpole, it was very kind. My family appreciates it."

"Colin, was there anything you want to ask us?"

"Can't think of anything right now. If he did it, I should be safe enough if he is going to prison."

"Knowing or suspecting isn't proof. We have arrested him, and I'm going to interview him now. Can you think of anything that might help, anything that might rattle him?"

"Not really, but Alison told me once that she wondered how her mum had died. She wasn't very old, but she remembered her parents arguing and then he told her that her mother didn't want her any more and had gone away to stay somewhere else. She never saw or heard from her mother again, and she thought her mum really loved her."

"Do you know where this was?"

"It was where that doctor was from, Keighley or Cross Hills, I think. She went and found her mother's grave when she was older. She said he would never talk about it at all. Alison never told him about finding the grave. She had been playing at a hockey match near there."

"We know he loves trains. Is there anything else he is interested in?"

"Porn, she said the house was always full of dirty magazines and videos."

"Anything else he didn't like?"

"He is scared of dogs and believes in ghosts; he is scared to death of them."

"Thank you. I'll come back and see you and tell you what happened. Do you have everything you need here?"

"Yes, thank you, sir; I even have a small telly I can watch. You will get him, won't you?"

James Boothby said, "Colin, I happen to know that Mr Catchpole always gets his man. I am sure he will."

"I will certainly try. If there is nothing else, we can do for you, we will go, and if you need you ever want to talk about anything, here is my number. I will be leaving a guard here just in case, not because I suspect you but because I need you to be safe."

Phillip Pickstaff was a large, almost obese man. He was suffering from a hangover. He seldom got that drunk, but something had unnerved him. When Saul and Geoff sat down to interview him, he wondered if they knew his daughter's ghost had come back to haunt him. He had seen her a few days earlier in the town and it had been a severe shock.

After the usual introduction, cautioning and clarifying identity, Saul asked, "Tell me how your daughter Alison died?"

"She got ill with some virus and died two days later."

"Which doctor attended her?"

"My old doctor from Cross Hills."

"Why did she not go to the hospital?"

"By the time the doctor got there, it was too late."

"It wasn't reported as a Sudden Death, why not?"

"He had seen her only a few days earlier."

"Mr Pickstaff, I think it might help if I tell you that Alison's body was exhumed and a post-mortem has shown us that she was killed by lethal injection, not by a virus. We have spoken to the doctor who certified her death, and he has admitted he only saw her after she had died and only had your word for what happened. He also told us why he signed the death certificate."

"You had no right to dig her up, no right at all."

"Actually, we did. I can produce the necessary paperwork if required. Did you kill her?"

"I never!"

"I think you killed her because she wanted to leave you and marry her young man. You couldn't bear that, could you?"

"I didn't want her to leave, no. He wasn't right for her. I needed her."

153

"When you were arrested, a DNA sample was taken from you. Your daughter was pregnant at the time of her death. We will be able to prove who the father of the baby was. Was it you?"

"She was a slut. It could have been anybody."

"Was it you?"

"All right, yes, it was. She came on to me. As I said, she was a slut, always wanting to go off with men. She was mine, mine!"

"It was both rape and incest and you know it."

"Well, it wasn't my fault."

"I am sure your solicitor will explain the law regarding that. Let us move on to something else. You met Colin Boothby by Alison's grave on Thursday twelfth of this month. What happened?"

"Who says I did?"

"He does."

"Liar, he is dead. You are a liar, and you are trying to trick me, to frighten me. That's your game, is it?"

"Well, how do you know he is dead?"

"I read about it in the paper."

"No, it has not been in any paper."

"Well, I just know."

"I can assure you that Colin Boothby is alive and has told us what happened. We know you had an argument with him at your daughter's graveside, and he threatened to come to us about how Alison died."

"All right, we did meet but I never killed him. Yes, we had a bit of an argument and a bit of a scrap, but someone else must have killed him when he got to the auction mart.

I want to consult with my solicitor without you listening, now?"

"By all means, but I will just put something to you for you to think about. How did you know he was attacked at the auction mart?"

Saul and Geoff left the room while Pickstaff spoke to the solicitor. An hour later, the interview resumed.

The solicitor said, "My client wishes to make a statement. But before that, he and I want to know firstly if Colin Boothby is actually alive, and secondly, he needs to know if his daughter is, in fact, dead because he believes he saw her in the street the other day. He also believes he saw her here in the police station when he was taken to his cell. What are you playing at Mr Catchpole?"

"Believe me; I am not playing at all. Yes, Colin Boothby is very much alive; my inspector and I spoke with him this morning. No, it was not Alison Pickstaff you saw here; I believe it might have been one of my officers. Geoff, could you ask WPC Woods to join us, please?"

A few minutes later, Chelsea came into the room and Phillip Pickstaff gasped and almost collapsed.

He stared at her and said, "It could be her. You tricked me into believing Alison had come back to haunt me. Now I think this is just all a trick and Colin is dead, I'm sure of it."

"No, this is WPC Chelsea Woods, who will stay for the interview. Now, are you going to give me that statement? I can assure you that Colin Boothby will give evidence. If you like, I can play the recording we made this morning to your solicitor. It has been typed up and is being signed by him right now."

"I thought he was dead. I was sure of it. Oh god, I had better tell you the truth then. He was trying to blackmail me. I followed him back to the mart and saw him about to make a phone call in a quiet place there, a huge empty room. I had to stop him, so I hit him with a bit of pipe I had found in a ditch near the graveyard."

"So, you intended to use the pipe before you even got to the auction mart?"

"I suppose so; I was just so angry; how dare he challenge me? It was his fault that Alison wanted to leave me. He encouraged her to challenge me. Me! She was mine! She was going to leave me and tell everyone the baby was mine; well, I couldn't have that, could I? All right, I admit I killed her. I didn't see any other way out. I got some stuff they use for heart problems from that doctor. He had to help me, you see; he was my wife's lover and knew if I told on him, he'd be finished. Alison was defying me, and I had to stop her. I knocked her down and I thought I had killed her then, but she began moaning, so I injected that stuff in the back of her leg. She died ever so quickly. The doctor agreed to sign the death certificate so he could be free of me."

"How long have you been having sex with your daughter?"

"Well, I started as soon as she became a proper woman, as soon as she got tits that showed, and she was mine. Oh, she used to try and defy me, but her opinion of me was never good, so it didn't matter what she thought.

She sometimes told me that what she wanted was important but of course, it wasn't. I told her that I had looked after her all those years since my wife left and she owed me for food, clothes and everything."

"How did your wife die?"

"She ran off with that bloody doctor but came snivelling back to me. I had to keep her locked in. Then she said she was pregnant by him. He tried to do an abortion on her, but it went wrong."

"We will come to that later. Tell me, what happened with Colin?"

"I hit him; he was unconscious. I smashed his phone; I admit I panicked a bit. I looked around and found an auction worker's coat. It was a bit small, but I put it on. I dragged Colin's body down the stairs and through the door at the bottom. There was a trolly nearby, so I put him in the trolly. They have auctions there for collectables, so I know my way around; I covered him with some empty feed bags I found, and then I wheeled him outside. The bloody trolley kept weaving all over the place, so it took a while. There were a couple of chaps outside, so I was careful, but neither of them paid any attention to me. When I got clear of the building, I wasn't sure what to do. I went over to the bushes on the far side of the car park and there was a big sheep lorry there. When I got close to the bushes, I could hear someone in there. Sounded like a courting couple and I needed to hide. Well, the only place to hide was in the lorry; there was a small side door in the lorry, so I pushed Colin in and then climbed in myself. It was full of sheep! I hate sheep. Then I heard whoever it was in the bushes come out and a girl said something like, 'Shit, that's my dad. He's seen us.' I watched through the slats in the side of the lorry as she ran away and the bloke with her followed her into the building. I slipped out of the lorry, hid the trolley over by the bushes and threw the pipe into the nearby ditch. I was going to get back to my car but then the chap who had come out of the bushes earlier was arguing with another man and I stayed hidden. The two men went off together. Then a couple of cars came in, paused for a couple of minutes and drove off again. I was going to make a dash for my car again but as I passed it, I saw the driver's door to the lorry was open and I saw the keys were in the ignition. I got in and started the lorry up and drove it out of the car park; I pulled into a layby bit further down the road, got out of the lorry and went back to where I had left the car, hid it in a nearby lane and went back to the lorry. I checked Colin's body was still there and then drove the lorry away. I couldn't dump him there; some of the drivers might have seen me."

"Did you see anyone you recognised?"

"No, I didn't. I didn't know what to do next, so I just kept driving; the bloody sheep were making a noise, so if I stopped, someone would have noticed. I drove for miles and stopped in another layby and tried to think what to do next. I found some brandy in the cab and drank it cause I needed a drink. When it got dark, I drove on, but I got lost. I ended up in the back of beyond. The sheep were bellyaching, thirsty I suppose. It was raining. I don't know what time it was, late, I think. There was this single-track road. I reckoned the driver would have reported the lorry

158

stolen by that time, so I didn't want to go on any main roads. I opened the side door to check Colin's body was there. It had rolled further in, so I leaned in to move it. Some of the sheep got out, so I opened the back up and let them all out. I had to let the ones on the upper deck out, too, because otherwise, they would have tipped the lorry over. I pulled Collin's body out and dumped it in some bushes. The road was too narrow to turn so I drove on. I had a couple of nasty moments. Once, I hit a wall by a bridge and had to reverse and get around a bend. Lights came on in a house nearby, so I put my foot down and drove on for ages. There was this downhill bit with a sharp bend, but the rain was tipping down and I missed it and drove off the road. I saw this gate ahead, so I drove through that and came to a stop in a clearing in a wood. I dumped the lorry there, then walked down the hill to a village and soon I knew where I was, Langcliffe. I came out onto the main road and walked into Settle. I got to the railway station there and managed to open one of the storerooms with one of my keys. I was careful not to damage anything. I caught the early train into Skipton, went and got my car and then drove home."

"Then you went away, according to your office?"

"You had no right to contact my office. Yes, I told them that yes, but I actually got some rest, had a clean-up, washed my clothes and then went on trip to the Lakes on the train; when I got back, I was in Skipton when I saw this woman here, and thought it was Alison's ghost come back to haunt me."

"When you were picked up, it was for assaulting a woman in Bradford."

"Yes, that slut she's a prostitute."

"I understand you use them quite often?"

"I have needs, more so since Alison died. I had to do something Sluts, all of them. She was trying to get extra money off of me; she wasn't even worth much."

"When you were at the auction mart, did you hurt anyone else?"

"No, I had no reason to."

"And no one spotted you?"

"No."

"So, you thought you had killed Colin. Why did you hate him so much?"

"He wanted to take my girl from me."

"What about her happiness? Did you not want what was best for her?"

"All women are sluts, they don't count."

"So, you are admitting to being involved in the death of your wife, killing your daughter and conspiring with Dr de Souza to conceal the murder and the attempted murder of Colin Boothby."

"Yes, I suppose I am."

"And incest with your daughter, rape and the theft of the sheep trailer and all the associated motoring offences?"

"Yes. I did not do any damage at the railway station, though."

"What do you expect to happen to you now?"

"Prison, I suppose; to be honest, I don't care."

"Can you describe the people you saw that day at the Mart?"

"Yes, I suppose so. I think the driver of the sheep lorry was the one in the bushes with the girl. He was a right ugly chap, and he had a cast in one eye. When he passed by me, he was doing up his flies; I dunno thirty, maybe forty. The girl was quite pretty but a bit chubby. She had on a rather dirty pink anorak and a very short skirt and high heels, pink ones. She was rather chubby, with brown hair with a pink ribbon in it. The man that met the driver in the car park was a stocky chap., He had one of those fancy carved shepherds' crook things, so I presume he was a farmer. He was wearing wellies, green ones blue trousers and they were filthy too. He seemed to be very angry; I saw him again later when I picked up the sheep lorry. He was at a barrel and was washing not just his hands but was throwing water all over himself. Then I saw him washing his hands."

"Go back to when you were in the corridor, when you were wheeling Colin out. You saw a couple of men; can you remember what they looked like?"

"Not really; one was young, he was whistling very badly, and the other was older. He had just come out of the gents; stocky chap wearing an auction mart overall. I didn't know either of them."

"What did you do with the coat you took?"

"I left it hanging on a hook in the sheep trailer."

"Dr de Souza says that you only agreed to have your wife back if she had an abortion and he says that you restrained her for it. Is that true?"

"Yes, she fought it; she didn't want the abortion, which is why it went wrong. It happened at his place."

"So, she was forced?"

"Yes, I didn't want the brat and he didn't want her."

"So, by restraining her, you murdered her too."

"I suppose I did. She was trying to call for help; I had to shut her up."

"Have you murdered or killed anyone else?"

There was a pause. Pickstaff looked at Saul and nodded. "It won't make any difference now, so I might as well tell you. Yes, I did. Again, I didn't mean to, there was this hooker down in Kings Cross. I go there sometimes 'cos I get free travel on the trains, see. It was about six months ago. I don't even know her name. I was waiting for a train to come home. I went out of the station, and she came up to me and asked me if I was looking for a good time. Typical whore, she tried to pinch my wallet after we had done. It was in some alley not far from the station. I lost my temper and hit her and as she fell, she cracked her head on a big dustbin, you know, the large industrial ones. Stove her skull in. She was dead 'cos I checked. I put her behind the bin and went and caught my train."

"Describe her; how old was she?"

"She was a black girl, not bad looking. About thirty, I suppose. She wore a gold chain. I got quite a bit for that; it wasn't like she was going to need it. She had some rings, too. They were too tight to get off her fingers. She didn't have no underwear, she was wearing scarlet, skimpy top and a very short skirt. She smoked and had bad teeth except for one gold tooth. That sort of fell out, so I took that too."

"You must have hit her very hard?"

"Well, she was trying to steal from me. I'd paid her fifty quid, and she wasn't worth half that. I took it back from a little bag she had. All she had in it was a key and some condoms and a syringe and her mobile phone; I threw that away."

"Would your fingerprints have been on anything, the bag or its contents?"

"I'm not that silly. I wore gloves; it was a cold night."

"Tell me, Mr Pickstaff, do you regret these things you have done?"

"I regret Alison, sort of. The rest were rubbish, anyway."

"Have you anything else you want to say?"

"Haven't I said enough?"

"Have you knocked any other women around?"

"One or two if they try to cheat me. That one last night, all I did was slap her around a bit."

"And that's all right?"

"They are just hookers, that's all."

"What would your parents think of what you have done?"

"I wouldn't even know; my mother was a prostitute and didn't want me. I never even knew who my father was, nor did she apparently."

"Is that why you hate women?"

"I hate all women; they all end up as tarts."

As they left the station a little later, Geoff said, "No matter how many times I meet evil like that, I can never get used to it!"

Saul replied, "I know. One wonders what turns a person into a monster. Can you liaise with the Met in London for me, please about this woman?"

"I will; you were never convinced this was all the same case, were you? I wonder what it is about that place that makes bad things happen there?"

"We have solved a bit of it, but we still have at least two more murders to solve. Mind you, what he did tell us was quite interesting and very helpful. Once he started, it was almost as if he was enjoying boasting about it. We had better find that trolley and the pipe. I'll get that started and you talk to the Met. We can leave the Cross Hills one for the moment."

Chapter 11

A thorough search failed to find the trolley they were looking for. The staff at the Mart agreed they were missing a trolley. They did find several feed bags with traces of blood on them. Saul found Des Trotter and Chelsea in the office there.

"Des, we need to find this trolly, any ideas?"

"Yes, sir, I have. I think I know where it might have gone. I'll go and check. I expect the local kids have taken it down to the waste ground where they play. They have a den down there."

"Before you do, can you tell me what Goodyard's daughter looks like?"

"He has three, but I take it you mean young Cherry. She is a bit plump, brown hair and the always wears a ribbon, almost invariably pink, a pink anorak, well it was pink when it was last washed, which might just have been when it was new."

"How old is she?"

"Not sure, fourteen, fifteen at the most. She's not over-bright, sir. I cautioned her for shoplifting from the village shop last year."

"Do you have a photo of her?"

"Not police one, no, but I can show you a school photo taken last year; I'll look it out."

"Please. Now tell me, do you know if Robin Goodyard had a decorative carved shepherd's crook?"

"Yes, it is a very good one. Quite showy."

"Now, I would like you to listen to the tape of the interview with Pickstaff. Tell me what you think."

"Yes, Chelsea was telling me. I'll do that now."

"Chelsea, have you ever seen Pickstaff before?"

"Yes, I have. I was shopping with Bridget in town. We were down near the railway station, and he started following us. Now I know why."

"Well, it certainly served a purpose. It unnerved him. What did you think of what he said in the interview?"

"To be honest, sir, I was shocked. I think I must have led a sheltered life. I have heard about such men, but now I believe they actually exist. He really didn't care about those poor women, did he? I think what shocked me most was that the only thing he did care about was not causing any damage to the storeroom at the railway station."

"I know. I've met a few like that, but each time, I wonder what makes them the wicked killers they become. No doubt some psychoanalyst can explain it, I can't. It is not my job to. I just have to catch and justly convict them. What happens to them after that is not my concern. I am glad I am not called upon to judge them,"

"You must find it hard, sir, sometimes, not to hate them?"

Saul sat down and said, "That is a very astute question. You have put the matter very well. I've seen a lot of hate in my time, and always it seems to turn in on the person doing the hating. It is a very destructive emotion. Very dangerous. You pose the question: do I hate them? I can't give you a proper answer. I despise them, yes, dislike them certainly, but I don't know about hate. I think hate has to be a personal emotion. One says glibly, I hate something or someone, but what we mean is usually something else. You are just starting in this career and already you are raising this question. If you want the advice of an old man not far off retiring, keep hate out of your life. I am not a wise man, but I have learned a few things."

"You're not old, sir!"

"Bless you, child, I feel it sometimes. How are you getting on with the Whales?"

"I'm loving it. They are so kind. I never had a lot of fuss, and it is nice to be noticed just for being there. The digs are warm, quiet and comfortable. I've started redecorating it. Bridget asked me to go to a WI meeting with her. Is that all right?"

"Jam and Jerusalem? Yes, if you want to. I know they are quite modern in their outlook and address a lot of topical issues. Tell me, Chelsea, are you being pestered by amorous young officers?"

Chelsea laughed. "A bit, but it doesn't bother me. I have no intention of playing the field and they don't know me at all. I am not going to be known as fast; I'd rather find the right man when the time comes."

"Wise woman. If it does become a problem, tell me or Des and I will get it stopped."

"Thanks, sir, I am supposed to go to a training day next week. Do I still go?"

"Of course you do. What will you be studying?"

"Offences against the person."

"Very topical. Are you managing to study at home?"

"Yes, now. I need to come in and look in the library to check some things out, you know, case law. Me and forty others using the same four volumes makes it a little difficult."

"Then, while you are on my squad, use mine. In my office, I think mine might be a bit more up-to-date anyway. If you promise to bring them back, you can take them home with you. I cannot let a probationer in my charge waste time fighting for the use of books that are sitting on my shelves. What questions do you have to research?"

"I've got them here, sir; I was going to the library later."

"Yes, I see, fairly basic stuff. Now, this question, they are looking for a fairly recent ruling; they want some depth, I can see. Come with me when we get back to the squad office and I'll copy what I think you need to read up on. I can hardly ask you to work the hours you are and not guide you a bit, can I?"

Once back at the Murder Squad office, Chelsea came out of Saul's office with a whole load of papers and several volumes of law books and she said to Des, "I never expected this!"

"Nor did I. He's determined to make the best of his staff."

When Chelsea got home that afternoon, she sat down and spread the books out and worked solidly for some time. Saul's suggestions had made life much easier for her and in a neat hand, she had completed the month's study. Bridget knocked on the door and came in with a pile of neatly ironed washing.

"You look busy, lass. Studying to be like that nice Mr Catchpole? I'll not disturb you."

"No, I've done for tonight."

"Then come in for a light supper. I warn you, we've a whole load of chicks hatched, and they are everywhere. Would you help me round them up? They are running around my kitchen floor!"

Chelsea enjoyed the next hour, and all the chicks were put in a suitable container, which Cyril took out to the barn. He came back carrying a small ginger kitten.

"I found this meowing up by the hay bales. It looks like it has been left behind or is the only one to survive. Shall I knock it on the head, or do you want it?"

Bridget took it and said, "Oh, poor little scrap. It looks old enough to survive. It isn't like we don't have two cats already. I'll ring round and see if anyone can offer it a home."

"I will if you will let me. I love cats. I was never allowed one at home. He is so cute! Do we have anything to feed him with? I'll pay you back and get some proper food tomorrow and I'll get him checked over at the vet."

They took the kitten through to her flat and after he had eaten a good meal, they equipped him with an earth box and found some old blankets to lie on.

Cyril said," What are you going to call him?"

"I hadn't thought. Let's see, red hair, male. I know, Saul."

"Saul it is then; keep him warm, fed and loved and he will be a great companion. We can look after him if you go away."

Saul, the kitten, began to purr in Chelsea's arms. A bit later, she cuddled him on the bed. Both fell asleep, very happy.

Isaac was a tall, well-built lad with freckles and dark red hair. He got off the train and was met by Jake and his father, who helped him with several cases out to the car park.

Jake said, "Hello lad, I haven't seen you since you were tiny. Don't bother with the uncle stuff; you can call me Jake."

"Thanks, I've been longing to meet you. I have heard lots about you and Uncle Saul."

"Probably all true. Your Aunt Anna is waiting for you, so we had best go. Is there anything you need to get before we do?"

"I need to buy her a present and one for Uncle Saul. It is really kind of them to invite me. Dad, what should I get?"

"Flowers would be nice for Anna but get Saul a decent corkscrew. His, I noticed, is almost falling apart. You and I need to talk, Isaac."

"I know, Dad. I am sorry. I've caused a lot of problems at home. I understand why you are letting me come up here; it is to give us both a break."

"It isn't that I don't love you, son; it is because I do. Please don't think I'm chucking you out."

"I know. Mum and I had a long talk last night. She explained. That was before Mal arrived and made her cry. Again. He told me I was coming to a wicked house where all tradition and respect had gone. It sounds cool to me. He then lectured me at length. Dad, he took all my CDs and stuff and my player and threw them in the bin and said you had obviously lost your marbles; he felt he had to step in as head of the family and lead me back to God."

"He said what? How dare he. Son, I am so sorry. I'll replace your things."

"You don't have to. I rescued them after he'd gone and cleaned them up. The players bust but I'll save up and get another."

"I'll get you one before I go. I owe you an apology. I did not see what he was really like until I was shown over the last couple of days."

"Thanks, Dad but you don't know the half of it. I shouldn't hate him, but I do. If anything could put me off religion, he has. Jake, I'm longing to meet your wife, Diana, isn't it? He railed on about her said she was the devil's spawn. Please tell me what she said to him?"

"Rather a lot, which was true. He didn't like it much. I said quite a bit, too. Your father will explain."

"I can't wait to hear! Dad and Mum sent a message. She wants you back as soon as you can. She is really scared of Mal. She asked him to leave yesterday, and he wouldn't. Ariel got him out, eventually."

"I'll ring her."

"Not on the house phone, he ripped it out. He said you had deserted us and told me if I came up here, I'd be deserting the family. It sounded fine to me, but I felt bad about leaving Mum and Rachel. He made Rachel cry, too. Then he told her she should be a wife and mother, not have a career. Are all elder brothers like this, Jake?"

"Saul never was if you remember Abe. He wasn't a bad elder brother at all. He got us out of all sorts of scrapes and usually covered for us."

"Yes, he was great. I'd sort of lost sight of that. One thing he never was a bully. Do you remember when he fought that thug, Vincent Pegg?"

"Oh yes, indeed I do. Vince was picking on us with his pals. They were squashing us into a corner and called it making Jew jam. Saul arrived and took them all on singlehanded and beat the lot of them."

"Yes, he lost his temper. After, he wouldn't say where or how he had got a cut lip and a black eye, although I know Dad pressed him. He swore us to secrecy about it; I think Saul was red in the face for days."

"Then there was that time when Mother found a bacon sandwich in our room. Mine, I think it was. He said it was his and Dad punished him for it. He was grounded for two weeks."

"Not to mention the time I broke that clock. Do you remember the fuss?"

"We were mucking about and knocked it over. Saul came in, got us out of the way and I think Dad beat him for it; he never squealed on us."

"That's right. Saul never held it against us. He was a great brother, wasn't he Abe? You'll like him, Isaac."

"I am sure I will. Mal always told tales on us if we did anything wrong. Dad, I have a confession to make while we are talking about this kind of thing."

"What?"

"You remember that picture that got broken, smashed?"

"Yes, of all of us on the Mount of Olives."

"Well, I broke it. It wasn't deliberate, but it was me. I felt awful afterwards."

"Yes, Mal told me you had done it. He went and got a new frame for it."

"No, he didn't. I bought it, and Mal took it and lied about who bought it. To make me look bad to you and him good."

"Did he now? Thanks for telling me."

When they arrived at Saul's house, Anna was waiting for them and welcomed Isaac warmly. She gracefully accepted the flowers he gave her and said, "Welcome, Isaac. Come on in. Your room is all ready for you. Abe, your wife rang and wants to speak to you as soon as you can call her."

Isaac looked in his shoulder bag and produced an envelope. "Thanks, Auntie Anna. Malachi gave me this to give to you."

"Did he? Oh, yes, the money I loaned him; where did he get it from?"

"My mother, I did ask her if it was all right with her, and she said yes, it was. Thank you for letting me come to stay. I'll try to be good."

They left the luggage in the hall and went into the kitchen; Abe and Jake took the luggage upstairs and while they were alone, Isaac said, "Aunt Anna, I need to say something; please don't bother with kosha food for me after Dad goes; I don't need it or even want it. Nor do I want to go to the synagogue all the time. Will Uncle Saul make me go?"

"No, he won't. He'll take you if you want to go, and he may even ask you to go with him on the very rare occasion he visits, but no, he is very fair. He is, however, head of this house and will lay down some ground rules which we both ask you to respect. He doesn't eat kosha food either but does not eat pork or bacon. That is up to you."

"I love bacon. Do you mean I can have it here instead of sneaking off to a café?"

"If you want it, yes. You know you look so like Saul."

"Yes, Mal said I'd fit in here, being an unholy argumentative rebel. Why did you ask me here?"

"Because I thought you needed somewhere to get your head together. Please don't think it is a soft option or that we are pushovers we are not."

"I never did. I respect both of you."

"Then, hopefully, when we get to know you, the feeling will be mutual."

Later, Abraham had a long talk with Isaac and then asked to talk to Anna. Isaac took the opportunity to go out

174

into the back garden and he played with the dogs and soon Jake joined him. "You all right, lad?"

"Yes, I think so. I've a lot to sort out. Dad said I could trust all of you and told me to respect you and especially Aunty Di. He thinks she is incredible, is she?"

"Judge for yourself. She'll be arriving soon and stopping for supper. She is a very clever woman."

"So, Dad said, He gave me lots of advice, but it wasn't a lecture. He said you and Uncle Saul have turned out very well."

"Generous of him, I'll also give you some advice. But it is up to you if you need it. Be true to yourself, have principles morals and stick to them."

"Thanks. I need to be me, not someone else that others want me to be."

"Sensible start."

"Is it true you have a farm?"

"Yes, a couple, actually."

"I know Aunt Anna is a teacher. I was hoping she might be able to advise me on what course to take. Jake, what did you do when you left school?"

"I followed Saul to university, got a rather mediocre degree and was bored, so I joined the Royal Navy, then I branched off, kicked around the world and ended up here. I met the love of my life and settled down."

"Is it true you have lots of children?"

"A few, yes. I've supported them all, but I am not a part of their lives. My morals were never good, and you should most definitely not follow me; I was very wrong. I just had not met the right person; I have now."

"I can't wait to meet her. Dad says there is some mystery about her, is there?"

"Does he now? If you want to know, ask her. She won't tell you but she'll spin you a good yarn. I will tell you that she has more brains than the rest of us put together, and she is very powerful woman."

"More than Uncle Saul? I thought he was the brainy one. He's very senior, isn't he?"

"Very. If he goes red in the face, keep out of his way, same with me, but your father never really had a bad temper."

"I have, though; I go red, too. This is a lovely garden; we don't have a proper garden in London. Just the park to play in. Jake, there is one thing: I hate the name Isaac. I would rather everyone called me Zach, would they mind?"

"No, Zach, good idea. I just heard a car pull up; we need to go in."

Before they could get back into the house Diana came into the garden to find them, she was accompanied by their huge dog.

"Di, this is Zach. Did you have to bring Hercules?"

"Yes, I did. He simply wouldn't get out of the Land Rover; Zach lovely to meet you. You look so like Saul it's uncanny. When you have settled in here, I hope you will come and visit us at the farm."

"I'd love to. I expected you to be ten feet tall, at least, Auntie Di. Anyone who can make mincemeat out of Malachi is a heroine to me."

"All I did was tell him a few home truths. Unfortunately, I have a tongue like a lash."

176

"My father thinks you are wonderful."

"Then he doesn't know me very well. I like him too. If you let Hercules dribble like that all over that immaculate suit, it will need cleaning. You must be all right; he likes you!"

"I love dogs, and I always wanted one. Maybe I can help by walking Uncle Saul's dogs. Are they really called Hector and Lysander?"

"Yes, and as Saul is working long hours, I am sure he will appreciate it."

After they had all had a delicious tea, they helped Abraham pack his things and load up his car. He then said his farewells and Isaac went out to the car with him. Isaac was startled to see tears in his father's eyes and gave him a big hug.

"Please don't be upset, Dad. Will you ring me when you have time and especially once you are back home. I will ring you or Mum at least once a week."

"Yes, son, I will. I love you. Please know that."

As Abraham drove out of the driveway, there were tears in Isaac's eyes, too. A car pulled into the drive and as Isaac watched his father drive down the road and was trying very hard not to cry, a soft voice said behind him, "It's all right, Isaac; I know it must hurt a lot. Come on in and we can get you settled."

Isaac turned and said, "Uncle Saul, thank you, and thanks for having me here; I'll try to be good!"

"I'd rather you tried to be yourself! I always found trying to be good a real problem. Things seldom turn out

177

the way you planned. Come on in and we can have a chat man-to-man. I can explain a few things?"

Isaac looked at Saul and said, "House rules, things like that?"

Saul grinned and shook his head. "Them too. It is best we both know how we stand. I am not going to lecture you; I think you have had enough of that to last a lifetime. Now, I need to open a bottle of wine when we get in. Which do you prefer? Red or White?"

"You are offering me wine? Wow, red, please."

"Well, you will have to learn to drink it sometime; come on into the study and we can chat there. You could easily pass for eighteen; here, if you behave like an adult, you will be treated as one. Just don't let Jake get you drunk. It's fun at the time but the hangovers get worse as you grow older. He has a huge capacity. The only person I know who can out-drink him and everyone else is his wife."

"But she's half his size!"

Saul took the opportunity of showing Zach around the house and explained that he would have his own bathroom and room and said he could use everything in the room. This included a computer, a television and to Zach's delight, a CD player. He offered Zach the use of several bicycles that were in the garage and by the time they got back downstairs to join the others, they were laughing happily together.

The next day, Saul had a day off and he and Anna took Zach out and arranged for him to join the local gym on the family ticket, and then enrolled him at the technical college, then they did some shopping, mainly to buy Zach some much needed casual gear and sports gear, and some new shoes including some trainers. They called in the local supermarket and Zach asked if there was a vacancy for a shelf stacker on a part-time basis and the manager interviewed him there and then. The manager explained that he knew Saul and Anna and had, in fact, employed both their sons in a similar capacity in the past. He was taken on for two evenings a week. By the end of the afternoon, Zach knew he was going to be very happy living there. He and Saul took the three dogs out for a walk in the local park and had great fun. It was as good for Saul as it was for Zach, giving him much-needed relaxation. It gave Zach the opportunity to talk about his ambitions and circumstances. As it was a hot day, they stopped by the lake and indulged in an ice cream, and while they did so, the dogs decided they wished to have swim in the lake. They enjoyed it so much that none of the dogs would come out of the water and obviously thought a swim in the deeper water was essential. They found the fountain in the middle of the lake great fun and refused to come away. Saul and Zach both tried to call them back and, in the end, the two of them had to swim out and fetch the dogs. They managed to put the leads back on the dogs and then they needed to dry the dogs and themselves before heading home. They walked in the sunshine until they were all dry enough to go home.

Chapter 12

Two days later, having followed up on the many enquiries to do with the murders, Saul came home from work and was looking forward to Jake and Di visiting for a meal. Anna and Zach had prepared a meal and by six, they were all sitting in the lounge feeling quite replete.

Di asked how the murder case was coming on, and Saul replied, "Much as you would expect but I think I need to talk things through with you to see if I can make some sort of sense of it. I think that we are dealing with more than one case, but both came together at the same time and place, and I don't know why. I would be grateful for your input, all of you. Maybe you can see what it is have missed."

"Uncle Saul, are you sure you want me to hear this? I mean, I am not a detective."

"If you don't tell anyone else what you hear, I would like your opinion. You look at things through much younger eyes. I welcome any thoughts. I ran something through with the squad the other day and the best idea came from a brand-new probationer."

Saul went through the facts of the cases as they were known and outlined the forensic results. He then said, "What I cannot get is how they are all connected; there must be something; it can't all be a coincidence, can it?"

"You say it all started when this boy, Colin, went missing?"

"Yes, Di. If he had not been missed, the bodies would not have been found for ages, or at least until the next day."

"Could anyone has seen this attack on the lad?"

"I suppose so. The window from the corridor to the bar looks down on the cattle ring."

"So, someone could have taken the opportunity to do what they did, hoping Pikestaff would be blamed for the lot?"

"Yes, but who and why?"

"Was that corridor locked?"

"No, but the bar was, so it would have been pointless anyone using it."

"Unless they were watching this Pickstaff man and also knew the building well."

"Good point, Zach. One I had not considered."

Di asked, "Who else who knew Pickstaff and knew the bar corridor would have wanted the lorry driver out of the way?"

"I'm not sure."

"Uncle Saul, was this lorry driver having sex with the teenage daughter of the farmer next to Colin's dad?"

"I have no idea."

"Then why not find out?"

"We will. I doubt they will be very helpful; they don't like the police at all."

Jake said, "Then get someone more her age to do it, a woman officer, maybe."

"Yes, young Chelsea might be the right one, but I don't want to put her in any danger."

"You mean you suspect her father and think he may be violent if he knows?"

"Yes, I do."

"Uncle Saul, was that farmer's son there that day?"

"No one has mentioned him."

"I'd want to know where he was. I know I don't know anything but if he lost this Alison girl to Colin, maybe he still had feelings for her. You said they fell out. Then he makes it up with Colin and didn't you say he knew Colin was going to meet the girl's father? I bet he knew where and when. Maybe he didn't like Colin that much. He might have followed and watched. If this driver was abusing his sister, might he not be involved? Maybe him and the father?"

"Good point, yes, Di?"

"You say two men, both strong, got killed. Would it not have taken more than one man to move the bodies? How did they get this auction worker in the ceiling, anyway?"

"We found some loose breeze blocks nearby and the body had been dragged in there. It was quite a tight fit. The ceiling tiles in the toilet roof underneath had been moved when, apparently, the body rolled off the joists in the ceiling and disturbed them. It was not as we first thought, pushed up from the toilet. It was dragged in from the corridor above."

"How big was this Yorke man?"

"Not very but he was stocky. I can look up his weight. He was a bit bigger than the lorry driver. Why?"

"Could we not try it, and see?"

"You mean to move a body in there?"

"Yes, I know it is probably a silly idea, but the reason I say it is I know how hard it is to drag a dead weight in a confined space."

"May I ask how Zach?"

"I am reasonably slim compared to Ariel or Dad. Dad has a huge store where he keeps ells and ells of tweeds and other clothes that are not used often. All the usual ones are kept on the upper shelves, but some of the Harris Tweeds and the unusual ones are stored at the bottom. There is very little room to move them, and they have to be dragged out. Sometimes, I need to help do it, and one of the other tailors comes and I go in and push and he pulls. Even then, it is hard work. There is no way, on the lower shelves, that I can do it alone. I've tried often enough."

"I should have considered that. I remember that store and doing just the same thing. Here, I've found the weights. Yorke was thirteen stone and Rees was twelve two. Zach, well done! I think we need to try this."

"Can I help Uncle Saul? I am just under twelve stone; do you want me to be the body?"

"Would you mind?"

"Not at all, it would be cool. Can I ask, when the body was stuffed in the roof, was there another way someone else could have got out?"

"I'm not sure. I don't want to make a complete ass of myself if there is a very simple solution. I'll ring William Atkins and ask if we could try it."

Di said, "Are you sure he is not involved?"

"Pretty sure, yes, I am certain his father is not."

"Then ring the father, Saul, not the son. To be on the safe side."

An hour later, they met Mr Atkins at the auction mart. Saul introduced his family and said, "Thank you so much for this. I trust I have not pulled you away from anything important?"

"Not at all. There is precious little I care to watch on the box, and this sounds intriguing. What do you need me to do?"

Saul explained what they wanted to test out and that if they were wrong, he would explore other avenues but wanted to see if their theories made sense.

Mr Atkins said, "Oh please, may I watch? The idea of such a senior detective as yourself getting stuck rather appeals to me. You obviously have a suspect in mind. Is it anyone I know?"

"We're not sure. Whoever it is has to have a good knowledge of this place, probably worked here in some capacity."

"Or still does. We have quite a few workers. Do you want me to find a list?"

"Would you? I don't mean full-time workers; we already have a list of those, but others such as electricians, work experience, plumbers, that sort of thing."

"I'll go and look."

Saul went to his car and fetched back several pairs of overalls from the boot. He handed one to Zach and another to Jake, who laughed and said, "Don't be daft! This might just go around my thigh, but not my waist or my chest. I'll risk getting dirty, thanks."

Mr Atkins returned and handed sheaf of papers to Saul. Saul glanced through them and said, "We'd better try this then. Come on, Jake, we'll see what happens."

Mr Akins found some folding chairs and Di, Anna and he sat at the bottom of the stairs and watched while Saul, Zach and Jake cleared away a number of the cardboard boxes. Behind the boxes was a wooden panel, which they lifted up to reveal a breeze block wall which had obviously been recently loosened. They neatly stacked the breeze blocks out of the way and revealed a hole in the wall. Zach looked at the hole and then asked, "Uncle Saul, where was Mr Yorke actually killed? Do we know?"

"Yes, we do. He was obviously attacked down the corridor there, in that bit by the door that leads up to the cattle ring. We found a bit of his blood there but not much. He was actually killed where we found him, on the roof."

Di asked, "Have we found the trolley that was used to move him yet?"

"You think he was moved by a trolley?"

"Probably, tell me, Mr Atkins, the trolleys you have here. Are they the ones with solid bases or mesh ones?"

"Solid, I can show you one. We have three; one is kept down here, but it is missing."

They went and fetched a trolley and Di looked at it.

"Yes, it wouldn't necessarily leak. What are they used for?"

"All sorts of things, moving tables, proven, old newspapers and stationery. The one missing from down here was old and needed replacing."

"Do you move dead animals in them?"

"Occasionally, if a sheep or calf dies or has to be put down. If so, they are disinfected and stream cleaned immediately."

"Do you know if that has happened recently?"

"Not for the last three or four months, no. As you so accurately asked, we found out a long time ago that the mesh ones leaked."

Saul handed the lists to Di and said, "Do you mind if we use this trolley for an experiment?"

"Not at all. This is fascinating; you think you have worked this out, Mr Catchpole, don't you?"

"It is just a theory. My nephew here is the one who thought of it. Di, where do we start?"

"By the back door, I think."

Anna began to video everything, and they went to the backdoor.

"Right, Zach, you have just come in; what and who can you see?"

"I can see the corridor as far as the bottom of the stairs. I can see Mr Atkins and Aunty Di quite clearly, even though the lighting is poor. I can't see under the stairs, though."

"Right now, someone has knocked you unconscious. Jake, you be the assailant. Hold Zach and carry him down the corridor."

Jake, who was an immensely strong man, picked Zach up and put him over his shoulder and walked slowly down the corridor to the stairwell and put him gently down by the hole in the wall.

Di said, "No, that won't do. Blood would have dripped. I assume the whole area was forensically examined? Try again, this time using the trolley."

They retraced their steps and this time, Jake put Zach in the trolley and wheeled it down to the stairwell. The trolley did not handle well and kept wobbling from side to side. Then Saul and Jake tried again, this time wheeling it together with one at the back and the other at the front, and it was much easier. Di pointed out, "Easier with two and difficult with one. If someone had been in a hurry, they might have knocked the wall with the trolley, so it took two to get the unconscious man here without leaving any blood traces."

"The only blood was here where Rees was lying. You can see the stains still, even though it has been cleaned up. If Rees was already dead, it wouldn't have been easy to move around his body. We really need another body."

"Allow me, Mr Catchpole, please."

"Are you sure, Mr Atkins?"

"If I am just to lie there, would you mind if I laid on a flattened cardboard box?"

"Good idea, yes, of course."

Zach and Jake flattened a huge cardboard box and helped Mr Atkins onto it. Saul gently positioned him and said, "Yes, that would be difficult. Try to get Zach from the trolley and into the hole without touching either Mr Atkins or the floor with him."

Jake tried several times but Zach either touched the floor or Mr Atkins each time. Saul stood back, thought for a moment and then said, "Let's both try it."

Once again, they wheeled the trolley to the stairwell picked Zach up. and managed to get him to the hole in the wall but had to put him on the floor before Saul climbed into the hole. Saul came out again and was relieved that he had worn the overalls as they were snagged while he had climbed in. He peered into the hole and then said,

"I am not large and there has to be another way without leaving a trace. Mr Atkins, allow me to assist you up, thank you. We need to have a rethink."

Mr Atkins returned to his chair and remarked, "This is fun! Thanks for the cardboard. It stopped me from getting too cold."

Saul stood looking at the flattened box for a few seconds and then said, "That's it! Of course. There were a number of cardboard boxes here that day. Some flattened, some not. Jake, try putting this one under Zach and then lifting him from the trolly and then into the hole."

Jake took the box and said, "Yes, I see what you mean. You'll have to get in first; here, use this plastic wrapping that is inside this box to cover the edges; it will stop any snagging. If we curl up the edge of the box, we can slide him in."

"Would it be easier if you came into the hole instead of me?"

"No, Saul, it wouldn't. I'm far too big. I know you don't care for confined spaces; Zach, I am going to slide you in feet first."

That did not work, as although Zach's legs folded up, no matter how hard Jake and Saul pushed and pulled, they couldn't get him into the correct position. Then they tried putting him in headfirst and this time, it took remarkably little effort and Saul laid on his stomach and pulled Zach to the area above the toilet. He then tried to sit up but was unable to. He pulled Zach into the position in which Herbert Yorke's body had been found. Zach's legs were a bit longer, but it proved it could be done.

"This is the only place I can reach around Zach's neck. I can't raise my arm far enough to strike him, so it means we have got it right. Stay put, Zach and I will try to get out over the top of you. No, I can't; my legs and body are too long. It had to be someone quite bit shorter than me. I am six foot two, Jake. How tall are you?"

"Six four."

"Zach."

"Six foot."

"Diana?"

"Five six, let me try."

Saul managed to get out with some difficulty and Diana, an experienced caver, slithered in easily and even managed to turn around.

She called back, "This is as far as I can go. I can see some way, but the girder is blocking me. I will come out and then you follow Zach; sorry if I am kicking you."

Once they were all out and had dusted themselves down, Mr Atkins said, "So, you have demonstrated that it took two people to put poor Herbert's body in there."

"Yes, someone smaller than me or my brother."

Diana peered into the hole and asked, "Saul, how did you get the body out?"

"Through the toilet roof. We replaced the tiles with new ones. Interestingly, we found not only Mr Yorke's blood but an unknown person's; it is being checked for a DNA match at the moment. Everything was photographed and measured, but no one actually tried it. Thank you everyone. Can we use the trolley, take it across the car park and then bring it back? Zach, do you mind?"

Together, Saul and Jake wheeled the trolley across the car park, and then Zach got out and they returned the trolley. Zach rubbed his leg. "Zach, are you all right?"

"That was a bumpy ride; I think I might have two or three bruises. Here on my leg, my elbow and my chest."

"I am so sorry. Interesting, Colin had similar ones. I owe you a drink, Zach."

As they returned the trolley and chairs and rebuilt the wall from the breeze blocks, Anna went and found a broom and swept away any rubbish and Mr Atkins thanked her.

He added, "I think this merits a drink; come up to the bar; you have certainly earned it. Mr Catchpole, you think you know who it is now, don't you?"

"Yes, I may be wrong, but it gives us a start. We need to check another couple of things."

"I can't wait. This is better than the tedious repeats on the telly. I think you also do not want me to tell anyone else?"

"I would rather you didn't."

"In other words, you don't want my son William to know; that tells me he is not quite in the clear yet."

"I have to be sure, I'm afraid."

"How refreshingly frank of you. Of course, you do; I have no reason to tell him about this. Do we have a drink before or after the two other things you want to do?"

"After. We need to go upstairs to the bar corridor first. Di, can you be Pickstaff and Zach can you be Colin? Jake, see what you can hear from the stairway."

Di loaned her Vodaphone to Zach and he went into the cattle ring and sat on an upper tier. Di followed him and he then laid down. She opened the door to the stairway and Jake came through and carried Zach to the base of the stairs.

Then they locked everything up and Saul asked, "What could you see from this window?"

"I saw everything until they went through that door."

They walked back through the cattle ring up towards the bar. Zach was about to give Di her phone back and paused and said," That's odd."

"What is?"

"I thought you said there is no signal here. It is full strength here, but I noticed down in the ring itself there was none. Colin could not have made a call from there. Who told him he could?"

Mr Atkins said, "If that is Vodafone, the young man is quite right. It works well at the front of the building. No phone works in the cattle ring, never has."

"Do all the staff know that?"

"Yes, we tell all persons in there that their phones will not work. I ask everyone to switch phones off during a sale."

"How well do you know Norman Ley?"

"More than I care to. Nasty little weasel, I never did like him. Lazy skiving, lad. Oh, he can work when he thinks you are looking. The moment he thinks you are not; he is having a sly fag."

"Do you know if he has many friends amongst the staff here?"

"Young Michael obviously, but yes, there was one lad who worked here for a while, John someone. I'll remember it in a bit. Farmers lad, but then most of them are. Stocky lad quite short, about five foot six, I would say. I do remember I was in the poultry ring with a fur and feather sale. It was hot, very hot. This lad was standing next to me; He stank of BO. I told him to go and do something else. I mentioned it to one of the auctioneers and suggested someone tell him to wash and give him some soap. I can't remember the surname offhand, but it might come to me."

"Is he on this list?"

"Let me see, no, no, no, not that one, no, oh yes, I remember John Goodyard. He left here four or five months ago. Now, what is everyone drinking? I insist on treating you in recompense for a splendid and interesting evening."

On the drive back, Saul said, "Zach, thank you so much. Thank you all. I have worked out now what I needed to know."

"I loved helping Uncle Saul, and thanks for letting me have a drink afterwards. I've never had a really good whisky before."

"Today, you did a man's job. You deserved it. While you behave like an adult, you will be treated as such. You have a sharp brain and a level head on your shoulders. I'm impressed."

Di added, "Not half as much as I was Saul. I know how much you hate confined spaces; you, Zach, did very well indeed. Fancy coming caving with me sometime?"

"I'd love to. I have always wanted to do that. Have you been caving with her Uncle Saul, Jake?"

Saul grinned. "Twice, she has been involved in cases with me where I had to go down a cave or a mine. I did it because I had to, but she apparently enjoys it. I do not."

"Really? What do you do, Aunty Di?"

"I'm just a farmer's wife, nothing more."

Jake laughed. "I warned you, Zach."

"Yes, you did. Now, why be so evasive about it?"

Di smiled and said, "I'll tell you one day."

"That sounds a bit like wait and see, which means never. I'll work it out; just give me time."

Saul was enjoying himself. "That's paid you back, Di; you usually say that to me."

"Yes, but what worries me is he probably will!"

Zach looked at the others in the car and said, "If you don't want me to know, then I expect there is a reason. All right, I'll leave it; thanks for a great evening anyway."

Chapter 13

The next day, the squad were very busy. Saul received the results of some forensic tests and DNA traces. He had a meeting with all the squad and briefed them as to the progress of the case. Each was told their specific tasks for the next day. Saul went to a magistrate and obtained several warrants and then made arrangements for the following day. He liaised with other agencies and spoke to the Footpath officer who had attended Goodyards farm. He then called in the help of the RSPCA. He went up in the force helicopter to see exactly where he needed to go and where to position officers. The helicopter observer turned and asked, "How are you doing, sir?"

"Callum Doyle! It is a long time since we worked together. I didn't know you were up in this thing."

"Not usually, sir, but I when heard you had asked for a jaunt, I wanted to come. The normal chap is off sick, so I volunteered. Tell me exactly what you need me to see and what you want photographed. I will be with you tomorrow and so it helps me too."

"Yes, I heard you had been made up to chief inspector; how are you keeping?"

"Father of two now and quite the family man! I sometimes work with your sister-in-law if needed, so I know you are kept busy. We sometimes use her farm for exercises; your brother is now a qualified pilot for these choppers. Did you know?"

"No, I didn't. So, I think, is she?"

"Has been for some years, so I understand, but she seldom flies them. Now, enough of that. How low do you want us to go and what exactly are you looking for?"

After the flight, Saul saw that everything was prepared for the next day, and he had an early finish. He and Zach went for long walk with his two dogs.

Long before the rest of the family were up the next morning, he left and drove to Des Trotter's beat house and issued him with protective clothing. They then drove to a rendezvous point a few miles away. They met Chelsea, Geoff Bickerstaff, Tarik, and Saul and briefed them all before they went to their allotted positions. Alan Withers had gone to interview Normal Ley, and two other squad members were interviewing Ted Atkins.

Saul took Des Trotter to one side. "I know you are not a police firearms user. I also need you to know that it could be very risky. You have a bulletproof vest on and a reinforced helmet but anyone of us could be hurt. Tell me, have you ever had any experience with firearms?"

"Well, I was in the parachute regiment for three years, so yes, I have; you asked if I was willing to come with you in the hopes, we could avoid injury. If I can, I want to. I know this family and we might just get close enough if I make the first move. They know me. I agree to come whatever the risk."

"Very well, thank you. I hope we are just being over cautious."

"So do I!"

Everyone got into position around the Goodyard's farm very early and waited. The daughter, Cherry, went to school in the usual taxi, which was stopped two miles away and then Julia Pellow took Cherry to a police station. Then, everyone watched as the mother left the farmhouse with the two younger daughters to take them to school. They were stopped out of sight of the farm and taken to the same place. There was a social worker waiting for them there.

Saul gave the signal to move in and walked with Des Trotter up to the farmhouse. They were not far from the front door when Robbie Goodyard came out of the door with a shotgun under his arm.

He recognised Des and said, "You again! What do you want now?"

"We need to talk. Can you put the gun away, please?"

"Who is this chap?"

"He's from CID. We need to clear up a few things."

"I've said all I want to, now clear off, I'm busy."

"This is important."

"Not to me, it isn't. Unless you have a warrant, get off my property!"

Saul stepped in front of Des and said, "Mr Goodyard. Here is a warrant to search these premises. I am arresting you on suspicion of the murder of Eric Rees and Herbert Yorke. Put the gun on the ground and walk forward."

Goodyard raised the gun and pointed it at him. He came out with a string of abuse.

Saul said very calmly, "If you don't drop the gun, you will be shot. You are already in the sights of several police marksmen."

Saul drew his handgun and pointed it at Goodyard, who looked rather shocked and then looked around and saw several marksmen within close distance. One was behind his muck spreader, and another behind his tractor. His bluster evaporated very quickly.

He put the shotgun down and raised his arms above his head. "Lie down with your arms out. Listen to me. If you move at all, they are instructed to shoot you."

Des ran and took the shotgun, broke it and removed two cartridges from it. The members of the firearms team came forward and handcuffed Goodyard.

Saul put his gun back in its holster and cautioned Goodyard and then said, "Where is your son, John?"

"He's not here."

"Where is he?"

"He never came home last night."

"Where is he?"

"I don't know and if I did, I wouldn't tell you."

Goodyard then called Saul and the other officers a string of offensive names and he was led away to a waiting police vehicle out of sight.

Saul called," Stay in place, please, everyone. I don't believe him, and the lad is here somewhere. Cover us as we go in, please."

Four of the firearms team went into the house through the front door and Saul followed, again with his weapon drawn. As he and Des got to the porch, there were two shots and the porch almost disintegrated around them. Des grunted as they both dropped to the ground.

Saul whispered," Are you hit?"

"Yes, sir, in the leg, I'm bleeding. Are you hurt?"

"Nothing serious." Saul dragged Des closer to the doorway and two more shots came from an upstairs window. Saul managed to shield Des and almost got him to the front door. They heard someone shouting,

"Let my father go, or I will kill the lot of you."

Saul called out, "John, listen. The house is surrounded; you cannot escape. He had the sense to give up; you have nothing to bargain with."

The reply was two more shots again from a shotgun, and pellets thudded all around them. Saul returned fire and shattered the window from which the shots had come. He then grabbed Des by the scruff of the neck and pulled him into the open doorway, reaching it just in time before a series of bullets thudded into the ground where they had just been lying. Saul knew they were not from a shotgun. He heard Des whispering a Hail Mary. He pushed Des into the hallway and one of the firearms team pulled him into what looked like a lounge.

Sauld followed and said, "Des, it's all right. We will get you out."

Des, who was biting his lip, said, "I'm sorry, sir. I'm scared. You must be, too; you're bleeding!"

"I think we both are. Now, where does it hurt most?"

"My left thigh, a bit above the knee."

One of the firearms team came over and produced a large wound dressing bound Des' leg and then said, "Where are you hit, sir?"

"See to PC Trotter first."

The volley of shots continued from the upper room. Then they heard a voice coming from a loud hailer trying to persuade John Goodyard to surrender and explaining that there was no way out for him. There was another exchange of shots.

The sergeant in the room with Saul and Des said, "Sir, two of us need to be at the door in case he tries to come down the stairs. Come further in."

"Is there a way out from here?

"No. The window is bolted shut and we are trapped."

"Is Des badly hurt?"

"Not sure, sir, let me see to you."

"No, I'm okay. God, what is that foul stench?"

"The furniture, sir. Don't touch it. The cleanest place is behind the settee, where we have pushed it forward. We now have to wait."

"Wonderful, we are no longer players in the game, just pawns trapped at that. I need to reload."

Once Saul had reloaded his gun and checked he was not badly hurt, he went over to where Des was lying behind the settee. Des was white, shaking and visibly sweating.

"Thanks, Guv, I reckon you saved my life. I'm sorry I lost it back there."

"You didn't. If must know you gave me strength; it helped me to know you were as scared as I was! Thanks."

They waited for what seemed an eternity while shots were exchanged intermittently. They made Des as comfortable as they could and raised his leg, and the bleeding had almost stopped.

Saul looked at the two officers who were stationed by the door and said, "You two need a break. I'll take over for a bit."

The sergeant said, "All right, sir, you take the left, I'll take the right; on my call."

They crouched almost motionless, ready to fire, while the other two officers went back into the living room and stretched,

Saul whispered, "I'm Saul Catchpole. What is your name, Sergeant?"

"Toby Hopkins."

"Well, Toby, it looks like we could be here for a while. Under the circumstances, you call me Saul if I may call you Toby? Are you scared? Because I know I am?"

"Yes, Saul, very, you train for this. You know what to do but never really expect it. It doesn't seem real, but it is. I keep thinking I'll wake up soon."

"I wish we could. Got a family, Toby?"

"Wife and one small daughter. How about you?"

"Wife, four children, two grandchildren and a nephew."

"We've another child on the way. Our little girl Mary is most excited."

"I have two grandsons, Benjamin and Saul both have red hair."

"My little girl is blonde, blue eyes, she is three. Maria, my wife, is blonde too but has grey eyes."

They spoke in whispers, mainly about their families, until they were relieved by the other two officers. Outside, they could hear a dialogue open up. They looked around the room for something to make Des more comfortable and found a rug and a cushion.

Des sniffed and said, "Thanks, but they smell foul. I'd rather do without, but as I am a bit cold, I must take the blanket."

Saul quickly took off his bulletproof best, jacket and pullover and then gave the jumper to Des. Toby contributed another jumper and a body warmer. Then Saul and Toby, having put their bulletproof vests back on, took over at door, and two more garments were added to help Des warm up. Once he was relieved at the door, Saul looked round the room and found an unopened bottle of rather cheap whiskey.

"Better than nothing. I can't find a clean glass. Here, Des have a swig."

They managed to get quite a bit of whiskey into Des and then listened to their radios. Saul produced a large handkerchief from his pocket, folded it and put it over Des' face just before the house was pelted with gas bombs. There was smoke and gas everywhere and a team rushed in through the front door and up the stairs.

There was a series of thuds from upstairs and then they heard. "All clear, one detained." They carried Des outside to a waiting ambulance.

Callum Doyle came over to them and said, "Are you hurt?"

"Not badly, is Goodyard uninjured?"

"Yes, just overcome by the gas. We waited until he was out of ammo, or we thought he was. May I have your gun, sir?"

"Yes, here. Six rounds fired, and it is fully reloaded."

"Yes, sir, that was my count."

"Please get Trotter to the hospital now."

"You go too, sir; that is an order from the chief."

Saul was pushed into the ambulance with Des and sat, getting out of the way while they tended to Des. Someone had wrapped a blanket around Saul and he suddenly felt a bit cold. The adrenaline had started to wear off. Des was still pale but remarkably cheerful. He admitted the whiskey had helped. Saul stayed with him until he was seen by the doctor and wheeled off to the theatre.

Saul was then seen by the duty doctor, who looked at him and said, "Why is it every time I am asked to see a police officer, you are involved? First, you try flying off a cliff, then someone whacks you on the head, then you have a car crash, and now you get yourself shot. For your information, I think your colleague will make a full recovery but will have a bit of a scar. He was more worried about you. Now let's have a look at you, shotgun, I assume. He insisted I gave you this bloodstained handkerchief back."

Saul had seven pellets removed from one leg, nine from the other and twelve from one arm. He was patched up, given some painkillers and released.

He was not surprised to see Chelsea come in the hospital with Aileen Trotter.

"Aileen I am so, so sorry. The doctors tell me he will be all right. He is in the theatre at the moment. What can I do to help?"

"You just have Mr Catchpole. You have told me he is not going to die."

"Do you blame me?"

"No, of course not. He knew it might be risky and told me he needed to be there. We all know the risks of the job; he certainly did. I brought some things in for him. Mr Withers offered me all sorts of help and Chelsea brought me here. She's been great. Please tell me he won't have to retire over this?"

"No, he is set to make a full recovery. He asked me to tell you he'll be out soon digging in the garden; I have promised him he can have a holiday before he comes back to work."

Once Aileen had gone up to the ward to wait for Des there, Saul turned to Chelsea. "Are you all right?"

"If you must know, I'm a bit shaken up, but okay. They are a lovely family and have good neighbours who are looking after the children now."

"I am sure, but I have a bit of a problem about you. He'll be off sick for a while, so I will have to put you with someone else until he gets back. Do you know Simon on the squad?"

"Yes, I do. I did an enquiry with him yesterday."

"I'll ask him to take you on, but I still need you on the squad and I think it is only fair you see this case through."

"Thanks; I had wondered when I heard Des was hurt. I might have to go to another station. I returned your books and things which were very helpful. My training day is tomorrow, and I am glad I got the work done in time."

"What's next month's topic?"

"Public order, poaching and the law regarding animals."

"I expect I have something regarding that, too, but I am not sure about the poaching."

"Des has things he says I can use. Can I give you a lift anywhere? Aileen is staying here; I'll pick her up when she rings me."

"Yes, thank you. Back to the office?"

"Surely you have been told to go home?"

"Yes, but I'm fine. I will when I know what has happened. I have only a few scratches."

"Whatever you say, sir."

No sooner had Saul got to his office than the chief constable walked in and said, "Home, now. I have been given an excellent report from several officers and you go home and rest. I also need to know how badly you were injured."

Saul said, "Just a few scratches, sir."

"I don't believe you. Either tell me, or I ring the force medical officer and get him here now."

"Very well, sir."

Saul admitted to having been treated with a number of stitches and to having some nasty bruising. The chief insisted on looking at his injuries and said, "As I suspected. Home, now. Do you need to be driven home?"

"No, sir, I am quite capable of driving." Saul picked up his car keys and left the office.

The chief turned to the officers in the room and said, "Typical. He was more concerned for PC Trotter than himself. His courage is an example to us all."

Saul arrived home to find Zach energetically gardening in their back garden with Anna. The lawn had been neatly cut, the flower beds weeded and the patio looked immaculate. Anna looked up at him and said, "I was just going to ring to see if you needed picking up from the hospital. Alan rang me and told me what had happened. He said you were walking wounded. Really, Saul, you are getting too old for these heroics. What's the damage?"

"Nothing much. What really annoys me is I have wrecked another suit. The garden looks nice."

"Stop trying to change the subject, but yes, Zach has done wonders. Come inside and when you have had a wash, we can have something to eat."

Half an hour later, Saul came downstairs and said, "Where is Zach?"

"He is such a nice boy. He probably thinks he is in the way. We had a very productive morning talking about what he wanted to do. Saul, can you find him and ask him to join us? He will accept it from you. I am so happy to have a youngster around again. It makes me feel young too."

Saul found Zach reading a book in his room. He looked at the book and said, "That was always a favourite of mine. Please come and join us; don't feel like an outsider."

"If you are sure, I don't want to get in your way. You need your time together; I know that."

"You mean your father told you not to intrude. You're not. As I said, you are part of this family now. Thanks for working so hard in the garden; tell me, did you walk the dogs because they look knackered?"

"Yes, I took them down to the park and we had a lot of fun; I do like those dogs. Aunt Anna said they growled at Mal; they are obviously wise dogs."

"Yes, they do have taste, especially if you leave edibles lying around; now I need your help. Once the news is on, I suspect my two sons will arrive expecting me to be at death's door. They will come to check. I need you to tell them I am fine. The girls are coming home this weekend, too and are longing to meet you. Sharon is your age and Susan just a year younger."

"It's Sharon's birthday on Saturday?"

"Yes, but she won't expect a present from you."

"I've already got one for her and a card. Aunt Anna said she likes Eminem, so I got her the latest CD. Were you hurt badly, I mean?"

"No, but one of my officers was. He is thankfully going to be all right, but I feel awful about it."

"I understand that. What can I do to help?"

"Nothing, no one can. Just relax, be yourself."

The rest of the day was hectic. As predicted, Saul's two sons arrived together with their wives and the two grandchildren. They immediately accepted Zach as one of the family and soon they were in the kitchen with Anna cooking a meal for the evening; then someone suggested a game of Trivial Pursuit and that was followed by games including Monopoly and one of Cluedo. Fairly early in the evening, Saul fell asleep and was gently woken. He made it up to bed while the family had a wonderful time. The next morning, Saul rang the office to be told that everything was in hand and not to return. He then went and fetched the two girls from their boarding school and the whole family had a party and a very relaxing time. Saul had, however rung Aileen Trotter to see if she needed any help. He spoke to the welfare department at his headquarters and arranged for everything she needed to be provided.

Detective Chief Inspector Alan Withers had taken over in Saul's absence. He sent Julia Pellow to interview Mrs Goodyard while another woman officer talked to Cherry with a social worker in attendance. The two smaller girls were taken to a place of safety until their mother could join them. The RSPCA were sent to the farm to check the welfare of all the animals there and with the duty vet, was able to treat several sheep, cattle and dogs for neglect and cruelty.

James Boothby came to the farm and spoke to them and then said, "I have spoken to a few of the local farmers. We can look after the farm for a while and get it cleaned at least. If you want to rehome that dog, I will take it, poor thing. I know when my lad comes out of hospital, he will take it on. I'll get the lads in to move the stock and once this place is clean and safe, we will return them and look after them until they are sold."

Soon, the farm was a hive of activity, and the stock was moved and well cared for. The dog was given a loving home at the Boothby's. Meanwhile, Cherry was interviewed and admitted that she had been raped on several occasions by Eric Rees. She also said she was terrified of her father and his temper. A detailed statement was taken from her.

The two young girls were also terrified of their father and their brother. It became very apparent from talking to the family that the farm was a place ruled by the father with a rod of iron. The interview with Mrs Goodyard was most revealing. She admitted that she had thought the murder of Eric Rees was down to her son and husband. She explained that she, too, was terrified of them. Then she explained that her husband gave her no money at all and did any shopping that was required. He had, many years before, stopped paying water rates and used only the rainwater collected in a series of tanks, which were mainly used to water the stock. There was no washing machine, no washing things or cleaning things, as he refused to purchase soap, saying they were not needed. They existed on the chemical toilet that he would empty into a pit. It was no surprise when the officer was told he had no sense of smell. Mrs Goodyard told the officers that she was never permitted in the barns and was told not to go near the dog. She and the family had been existing on the vegetables grown in their garden, which she was expected to tend, and what meat she had was from the farm. She had made all their clothes except the school uniforms, using and reusing the same garments to hand down to the children. He even resented her asking for thread, which he would buy and if he did so, it would be the cheapest available.

When it was explained to her that neither her son nor her husband would be coming home, she burst into tears and said, "Thank God for that. Do I have to go back there? I never want to see the place again."

There followed a consultation with the Social Services, the local council and all the families were examined by a doctor. The injuries found on Mrs Goodyard confirmed that she was regularly beaten. It was arranged for temporary accommodation for them, and they were asked what they wanted to take from the house.

She said, "My sewing machine, what was my mother's, please and we will need some clothes and all the essential things. I will tell you where he kept his money, he thinks I don't know. It looks bricked off, but it isn't. I don't know how much he has in there, but we will need something to live on until I can get some sort of a cleaning job or something. I'll tell you something else too. It was only when Cherry stopped asking for sanitary towels that he suspected she was pregnant and beat her to tell him who it was. It was only about two weeks ago he found out. I'll give evidence if you need me to. I tried escaping many times, but he caught me every time. John was just the same. We only had electricity, so the milking machines could be used. We don't even have a telly or a radio. Oh, John had a telly in his room but we weren't allowed to watch it. The TV people came once but they couldn't find where he had hidden it."

"Have you anyone else who could help you, family?"

"I have a sister; she lives over in Settle. I wasn't allowed to speak to her; I think I have her address. I know she would help me."

It did not take long for them to trace the sister, who immediately came over to the police station and offered to do what she could.

As soon as the search team went into the house, they needed to wear masks. The stench was terrible. Mrs Goodyard came and showed them various places she knew that things had been hidden in. Once she had taken what she needed, she went to a safe house and from there to a council house, where she burst into tears when she discovered it had hot running water, a bath, and even better, a washing machine. The officers left her in the capable hands of the helpers and were delighted to reunite her with her three daughters. The searching officers found a huge sum of cash hidden where she had said and were able to provide her with enough to last until things could be sorted out. They asked her what she would do with the rest of it.

She said, "I'll open a bank account and then he can't get it. Thank you, all of you; you have given me and my three girls our lives back."

When Saul went back to work on the Monday morning, Alan brought him up to date. When Saul and read all the statements, he turned to Alan and Geoff, who were in the room and said, "One wonders in this day and age how this can happen. Do you know if the farm is in his sole name or jointly owned?"

Geoff said, "We found the deeds; it is actually her farm left to her by her father; he doesn't own it at all. She has asked us to put it on the market. Can we do that?"

"We can't, not as such, but we can put her in touch with the appropriate solicitor. Actually, I think I know someone who might buy it. Ring this chap and see if he will deal with the legal stuff. As the money was in her property then it is hers. Let her put it all into a bank account. Now, can I read what the older Goodyard had to say?"

He was handed a typewritten statement.

I suppose I had best tell you all about it. I never liked Boothby; he was a bloody nuisance, kept poking his nose in and made a fuss if any of my stock got out. Then John told me about Colin, how he had got drunk one night and John suggested it would be a good wheeze to watch and see. I took some lambs into the sale; I dropped John off. I knew that Cherry was pregnant and got out of her who it was. That low-life Eric Rees. I decide who she sees, not her. I knew he would be there he usually is. I thought Cherry was at school. Then John told me he had seen what Pickstaff had done, and it was an opportunity we couldn't pass up.

I decided to deal with Eric and then we could get Pickstaff to take the blame. Then I saw Cherry and she was with Eric. I was so angry I saw red. We got him inside the mart in the corridor by the door. We beat his head in. He was a tough bugger, though, and took us ages to finish him. John told me about the hole behind the wall under the stairs. Then this old man saw us, so we had to shut him up as well. We put him in the trolley and got him to the hole but once we had pushed him in, well, John dragged him in, he started to come round. I gave John my knife and told him to finish him like you would cut a lamb's throat. Or a pig. Then there wasn't room for Eric in the hole as well, so John managed to get out and we were covered in blood. We had to hide him as best we could and covered him with boxes. There was a bit of that bubble wrap stuff that we had to use to slide the old fellow in, so we took that out with us, and it was covered in blood, too. Then we put the trolley in my trailer, John buggered off and I went and washed the worst of the blood and mess off me in the water but before I went back in the gents and had a better wash. I don't mind washing if someone else is paying for it.

I've been a drinker all my life. The doctor tells me I am dying of liver disease. They gave me six months that was four months ago. They said it might be longer if I gave up drink and fags, I won't. You will never get me to trial. John started to defy me, so I didn't care what happened to him. It was actually his idea to kill Eric. I was just going to make sure he never walked again or had sex again. So far as I am concerned, my wife can sell the farm do what she wants. Cherry would be better off with an abortion, but that's up to her. At least in prison, I'll be cared for looked after. They have to, you see. I must admit I never thought you would work it out; you might have suspected me but not John. We were so careful not to leave traces. Just make *sure that Boothby doesn't buy my stock, get them sold but not to him. The guns now they are well hidden. Trotter took my licence away some time ago. Bright chap Trotter, I never liked him much, but he was always fair. He did his job, I suppose. I'll plead guilty if I ever go to court, which I doubt.*

Saul put the statement down and then listened to the tape of the interview with John Goodyard.

"Why can't you leave us alone? You've got Dad, and now you've got me. OK, I took that dirty child molester out and he deserved it. We didn't want to take Herbert out, but he had seen too much. Can you actually prove I took Herbert out?"

"Well, we have your blood and DNA, with that of Yorke found in the hole where you put him."

"Damn it. It must have been from the cut. I nicked my arm when I cut his throat. There was very little room in there. OK, so you got me. You know I was going to have the farm when Dad died. He told me it would belong to me."

"Did he also tell you that the farm actually belongs to your mother, not him?"

"No, he didn't. She won't want it I'll get it from her."

"And how will you do that?"

"She will do it for me."

"She has already taken steps to sell the farm."

"Oh. I need some money through."

"I suggest you write her a letter asking for it then. She has already told us she wants nothing more to do with you."

"Writing isn't my strong point."

"Tell me, John, how did you know about the hole in the wall at the mart?"

"I worked at the mart for a bit. Didn't like it much, but I did become mates with Norman, Norman Ley. He told me about it."

"So why did you hate Colin Boothby?"

"I always have hated all that family. Dad does, too. They made such a fuss if one of our walls went down or a fence fell over. What I hated most about Colin was he pinched the girl I fancied. Alison. I met Colin in the pub one evening. I decided to get some information out of him, so I got him drunk. He, stupid boy, thought I had forgotten how he pinched her. He told me how he suspected Pickstaff had done her in, and he was going to meet him. He even told me when and where. I got a lift and then followed the silly boy. He looked a right pratt carrying those white flowers. I watched them in the graveyard, having quite a row. The Colin left and I saw Pickstaff was following him, so I did too. They went back to the market. I heard him ask Norman where he could make a phone call from as he couldn't get a signal where he was. He said he wanted to phone the police. I watched as he went into the cattle ring and Pickstaff followed him. Then I watched Pickstaff attack him in the cattle ring and drag him down to the corridor. He had picked up a bit of piping from somewhere. I saw him dragging Colin and then I went

215

round and spotted him wheeling this trolley. I saw Dad coming out of the mart. I told him what I had seen, and we found the piping. The dad saw Cherry coming out of the bushes. She was supposed to be at school. Then we saw Eric coming out of the bushes doing up his flies. Dad went for Eric's big style. I found the trolley in a ditch, and we wheeled him back into the building past Eric's lorry. Eric didn't go down without a fight. I had to hit him a few times with a bit of three-by-four. We finished the job by the bottom of the stairs. We were trying to push him into the hole when Herbert came along from the storeroom. He saw what we were doing and was about to raise the alarm, so we had to finish him, too. He ran like frightened rabbit. We caught him by the door. I got the trolley and put him in it. When we got to the hole in the wall, we used cardboard to slide him in, but he started to come around, so I had to get in there with him. Dad handed me his knife and said to finish him like you would a pig. That's when I nicked myself. Just as I was bricking up the hole, I saw a light come on, someone with a torch, I think. We put the panel back and l legged it out of there. We took the cardboard and some plastic stuff, and the trolley was covered in blood. We put it in Dad's trailer and Dad said to make myself scarce and to try and find Cherry. I did about half a mile up the road. Dad picked us both up and we put the trolley in the hay barn. It's been quite useful. We burned the cardboard and the plastic. Dad asked Cherry why she was with Eric, and she said he had paid her lots. We didn't tell her what we had done."

"OK, I admit I killed both of them and was glad to kill Eric, but I was a bit sorry about Herbert. He was always all right with me. I suppose I'll go to prison, and I hope I eventually go to one where I can be a farmer again. They have them, don't they? At least Dad won't have to go there. Tell my mum I want the money dad hid."

"Why did you shoot PC Trotter and the other officer?"

"I don't like coppers. I hope I really hurt them."

"Yes, you will be charged with attempted murder of both of them; they will, however, make a full recovery."

"Pity, oh well, I might as well be hanged for a sheep as a lamb."

"Anything else you want to tell us?"

"Only that, I hope you got electrocuted when you searched the place, 'cos we took the power from the mains. What I want to know is how you knew it was my blood."

"You were stopped for drunk driving two years ago and we took a DNA swab then."

"Oh yes, I'd forgotten that. I'd better tell you it was me who nicked the tractor than last year up near Ripon, a Ford one."

Saul moved on to the statement that had been taken from Norman Ley.

I lied when I said I had helped Colin Boothby. I knew he couldn't make a call from the cattle ring. John Shityard and I were mates. I knew he hated Colin. He told me later that Eric Rees had got his sister pregnant. I rather like Cherry. I also knew Mr Ted had been in the mart that day and I know why. He'd left a load of money in the first aid

217

storeroom. I didn't take it because it was the Euros. I knew
he was pinching money from the firm; good luck to him.

Once he had been brought up to date, Saul called a meeting of all the squad.

He said, "Well done, everybody. I am sorry I was out of it for a couple of days, but I think we can congratulate ourselves. We have solved three murders, possibly four, arrested the culprits, and stopped a massive fraud. I am delighted to tell you that Des Trotter came out of the hospital this morning and is on the mend. That is the good news, but I am afraid I have some bad news as well. Our office manager, Fred Dunlop, has taken a turn for the worse. His MS has got really bad, and he won't be able to return to work. He is moving into a nursing home. The prognosis is not good. He says he will be delighted to see anyone who wants to visit him. I certainly shall and I hope you will too. I understand his favourite is Talisker, but Glenfiddich will do. Paddy will be taking over the office. I am asking Caroline to come in and help arrange things. Over to you, Alan…"

"Yes, I also have some news. As you know, Caroline is expecting. She and I need to tell you that once the baby arrives, she will not be returning to work. She will be resigning."

"Thank you, Alan. We will be very sorry to lose you, Caroline, but we fully understand."

"I will be sorry to go, but a family is what I have always wanted, and I can't do both. We do want everyone to keep in touch though."

Saul smiled and said, "I expect we will all come to the christening if invited?"

Caroline replied, "Oh, you will be. Incidentally, it is a boy."

Chapter 14

Chelsea came and found Saul later in the week.

"Sir, thank you. I got top marks for my work on the Offences against the Person. They say my stint here is obviously doing me no harm. I am the envy of many of my peers. I saw Des yesterday. He wants to see you if you have time. He is much better, even walking around with a stick."

"I am relieved to hear it. You have done very well, Chelsea. Are you upset over what happened?"

"No, not really. To think that creep actually asked me out! I have settled in with Bridget and Cyril and I have started making friends. I even have a kitten!"

"I like cats, what kind?"

"A ginger male. He is great fun, very playful."

"What have you called him?"

Chelsea blushed, "I've called him Saul, I'm so sorry."

"I'm flattered. Red hair is quite understandable. I am afraid you might find ordinary police work a bit dull after this."

"I doubt it. I have so much to learn. Training department says this will have to be my CID attachment. I couldn't ask for a more exciting one."

Saul called in to see Des Trotter the next day. He had the usual welfare gifts. Aileen answered the door.

"Hello, sir, do come in. Tea or coffee?"

"Coffee, please, how are you coping?"

"Fine. I'll be glad when he gets back to work. He's fratching already to get out into the garden and out and about. The villagers have been wonderful, coming with gifts, offering help and keeping him amused. Go on in; I'll bring the coffee in."

"Before I do, I bought these for you."

"What beautiful orchids. How lovely, how kind of you."

"I grew them and hoped they might cheer you up. You've been through the mill, too."

Des was sitting in an armchair when Saul came in. Saul said, "Don't get up, man; here these are for you."

"Fruit and whiskey, eh? Thanks, and thanks for coming to see me."

"Can I help with anything?"

"It's not that. I want to say something to you. You saved my life, sir, and I know it. You may say you didn't, but you did. Thank you from the bottom of my heart. Here your jumper. Aileen washed it and mended the numerous holes in it. We took out nineteen pellets; I have them here in this matchbox if they are needed. Please take them. I doubt you can wear the jumper for anything but gardening, though!"

"Thanks, Anna knitted that for me. You needed it more than I did. So, how are you doing?"

"Very well. It is healing very nicely. The doctor is pleased. I should be back at work in a couple of weeks, but it might have be light duties for a bit. Chelsea says she is being looked after. I had Mrs Goodyard in to see me yesterday. I hardly recognised her; she was clean and fresh. She told me a lot and that she is selling the farm and never wants to go back there. Oh, and I had a long chat with Colin Boothby, who was on the same ward as me."

"How is he?"

"Still suffering from occasional headaches but on the mend. I thought I should tell you he has fallen for one of the nurses; she seems quite taken with him, too. I think it is not just his body that is healing, but his soul as well."

"Poor lad, but as you say, this might be a good thing; now, do you want to know about the case?"

Robin Goodyard died in the prison hospital three months later. Saul attended the funeral at the request of Mrs Goodyard.

As they left the churchyard, she came over to him with Cherry and said, "Thanks for coming. I wanted to say I don't bear any grudges. You did the right thing. I will tell you I want nothing to do with John, he always was as unbalanced as his father. I sold the farm for a very good price. Did you buy it? Catchpole is an unusual name."

"No, my sister-in-law bought it. She farms with my brother. She is hoping to find a good tenant. She also bought the stock. And the dog has been found a loving home."

"Good, I am grateful. Cherry is, too. We have now got the help she and the family need., that Robbie would never allow. She is putting the baby up for adoption and will be going back to school. Will you come to the Talbot Arms with us now? I've laid on a bit of a spread; we want to start and new life and now we can."

"I am not family; I wouldn't want to impose."

"We asked the Trotters too. We would like you there, you see we have no friends locally. Robbie saw to that. We also asked the officers that helped us so much after you arrested Robbie and John. It would comfort me to know that you wished us well. Most of the folk here today are from the farming community and all of them have helped us in some way. The Boothby family are over there. We don't want to leave no enemies, see. We have moved to Settle near my sister, and I have a nice house and I have a job as a housekeeper and the Golden Lion, Mo, the boss, asks to be remembered to you."

"Yes, I dealt with a case there. Thank you. I should be delighted to come."

At the hotel, he met many people who had helped in some way during. the case. He had a long chat with the Boothby family and they also thanked him. He chatted to the Trotters and several officers who had been involved in some way. He left after about an hour and took the rest of the day off.

When he got home, his daughter Sharon was practising the piano. Anna looked up at him and said, "You're home early for a change. Zach will be in soon and he wants to talk to you."

"Is something worrying him?"

"I think so. He and the girls are going around as if something awful has happened. They won't tell me."

A bit later, when Saul was in his study, Zach came in and said, "Uncle Saul, can we talk?"

"Of course we can. Are you in trouble? You look like a condemned man. It can't be college. I read your report and you are doing very well."

"No, it's not that; I've done something stupid. I expect you will send me away. I'm sorry, but I lost my temper."

"Go on, this sounds serious."

"You see, the girls and I went shopping in town two days ago. We went on the bus. Aunt Anna said we could. We got some things for Aunt Anna's birthday. We had a coke at a café and came back on the bus. There were a group of kids who go to college with me on the bus, at the back. They thought it was really funny to make nasty, rude comments to and about me and the girls. They are the right troublemakers at college. Always having a go, calling me names. I can cope with it; I just ignore them. We got off at the park because we knew they would be getting off at the stop round the corner and I thought it was the sensible thing to do. To avoid trouble."

"Very sensible. Just what names were they calling you?"

"Mainly ones about my being Jewish. I have never made a secret of it. I am what I am. I never told anyone, but one lad from the synagogue must have told them about Mal. They pick on that lad, too. They were chanting things like Jew Drop, Yid that kind of thing, very childish. Then they started being very crude about Sharon and Susan. Anyway, we got off and were walking back by the park and came in through the alleyway and they were waiting for us. They called the girls Jewish whores, and I am afraid I lost my rag, The biggest one, whose name is Charlie

Biggs, was spoiling for a fight. He got hold of Susan and asked for a kiss and tried to kiss her. I pushed him away and told the girls to run and I thought they had; the lads went for me and we had quite a fight. I really hit Charlie Biggs hard on the nose and then chased the others away."

"That sounds quite reasonable to me."

"That's not the worst part. I found out yesterday I'd broken his nose and knocked two teeth out, and I heard he was going to complain to the police about it. What I didn't know was the girls hadn't run away. They had come back and seen it all. Does that mean they were accomplices? I've caused trouble and I am sorry. Do I pack now?"

Saul looked at the anguished face of his nephew, noticing the bruising and a cut lip.

"No, you do not pack. This is your home. I can see some injuries, have you more?"

"Yes, loads of bruises."

"How big is this Charlie Biggs?"

"Bigger than me. He is studying mechanics at college, I think. He's fat, boasts that he boxes a bit, he can't much, or he wouldn't be so overweight."

"How many were there in this group?"

"Five lads and a couple of girls who were great at the name-calling but backed off when it got physical."

"Let me tell you something. The law allows you to defend yourself. The girls are not accomplices. They are witnesses. So, you broke his nose. We can deal with it. I'd have done the same thing, I think. In fact, I did once. I was walking a girl home in London. She was a neighbour, and these drunks were pestering her. She was very scared, so I offered to walk with her. These drunks were trying to touch her up and wouldn't leave her alone and threatened me if I interfered. One of them hit me, so I hit him back. Then another one hit me and then another one. One got up for more and I saw red and hit him until I didn't think he would get up again. I broke his nose and I think, his jaw. I saw he was spitting out teeth and blood. I took the girl to her door and went down to the police station and handed myself in. They picked up the drunks, spoke to the girl and two other women who had been assaulted by them, and then spoke to several witnesses that I had not realised saw it all. They prosecuted them. The inspector warned me about going over the top, took me home and told my father he should be proud of me. The girl's parents were very grateful. I did learn a lesson about going over the top, but now, I will thank you for protecting your cousins. Stop worrying, Isaac. I am not angry with you. This can be sorted. Maybe you did go a bit too far but so did they. Racial abuse is not tolerated, and I am going to call the local police here and explain what happened. We will make a complaint, not wait for you to be arrested. Let me talk to the girls and stop worrying."

The policewoman who came out to see them later that day listened carefully to what was said. She took statements and a copy of the video that Susan had wisely made of the whole incident, including the abuse on the bus and arranged for Zach's injuries to be photographed.

She made a list of the names of those involved and said, "I've dealt with Biggs before. I happen to know he is a member of the National Front and the last time he beat someone up, it was a Muslim girl and her little brother. He has not yet made a complaint about this. If he does, I will let you know but it sounds like self-defence to me."

"Will I get a record? You see, I want to join the police and be like my uncle."

"That I can well understand. As a matter of interest, do you box?"

"No, but I would like to."

"My partner coaches at the local sports centre. Why not go down and see how you get on? You obviously have quite a right hook."

"I'll ask my uncle if I can."

When he asked Saul about it, Saul said, "This is not my decision. I think we need to ask your father if he is agreeable. Personally, I think it would be a good thing, but the decision must be his."

Saul rang Abraham and explained, and Abraham surprised both of them and agreed for Zach to learn to box.

Then Abraham said, "I need your advice, Saul, and I need to talk to both of you. Can I come up with Ariel?"

Saul looked at Zach, who smiled and nodded. When the telephone call had finished, Saul asked Zach, "You like Ariel, I think?"

"Yes, he is all right; he is a bit serious sometimes but has often stuck up for me and Rachel. Dad likes him because he wants to go into the business. He is already pretty good at it."

"Would you mind sharing your room with him when they come? Jake and Di are staying, too. Of course, the girls are here during the holidays, so your father can have the other room. He says he needs your advice too."

"Why would he want my advice? I'm just a kid to him."

"Not any more. I've told him how mature you are, how industrious. You've been no problem."

"You mean when I am not breaking the greenhouse glass with a football or falling into the fishpond."

"Well, apart from those times but I did worse at your age. So did your father, but I doubt he's told you that. I remember once he decided to climb up the drainpipe from the backyard. I never did find out why. Jake probably dared him to, anyway he pulled the whole thing down and the guttering and quite a few slates from the roof. Jake caught him as he fell, and the crash was quite horrendous and there was mess everywhere. The cast iron drainpipes and guttering smashed into a thousand pieces. The cycle store roof was smashed. I got there just in time before Dad. My mother was having hysterics and Dad was livid. We all got punished, beaten actually, and then had to work in the shop for ages to pay for it."

"Why punish you?"

"Because I was the eldest and should have been looking after them. It was a bit unfair, but I was studying hard, and it was simpler not to argue. We stuck together as boys."

"Was Grandad very strict?"

"I thought so at the time. Being the eldest had both advantages and drawbacks."

"He never talks about you or Jake, why not?"

"Well, he never forgave me for not marrying the Jewish girl he had picked for me. I couldn't. I was already in love with Anna. That woman was ghastly! Oh, she was a handsome girl, but she was also a shrew. Bossy, controlling, lived for money and jewels. She assumed I would go into the family firm and be rich. I think father told her I would. Mother understood we kept in touch quietly until her death. Father disowned me years ago, even returned letters and cards I sent to him. I have tried to open up channels of communication, but he doesn't want to know me. Won't even see my kids."

"That must hurt like hell."

"It does but I am still trying."

"You don't think my dad wants to see me to make me marry someone he's picked, do you?"

"No, of course not. He couldn't, wouldn't. If he did, I would stop it."

"Thanks, Uncle Saul. I'll go and make up the other bed for Ariel now and help Auntie Anna do the one for Dad or do it for her. I'll tidy my room too."

"Why? It always looks immaculate on the odd occasion I have been in there. You are the tidiest chap I know."

"Not according to Malachi. I only got that way to hide things I didn't want him to see."

"I trust you don't feel the need to hide things from us?"

"I don't need to; you don't disapprove of everything I do."

"Not at all. Tell me truthfully Zach, do you want to go back with your father?"

"No way! I love them, yes, but I can breathe here. I've started to make friends here and college is good. I can do my sport and I love you all. I hope I am not in the way?"

"No, you are not. Anna said only yesterday how happy she is that you have settled in. Do you want to invite these friends back for a meal or to play music? You can you know?"

"Really? They are not Jewish."

"Of course you can. I don't care if they worship tadpoles so long as they treat my house with respect."

"Tadpoles?"

"Never mind, it's something Di said to Malachi."

"I must ask her. I do like her and Jake. I've worked out, I think, what she does, and I'm impressed."

"Have you now?"

"Yes, I think it is something like MI5 and I think you and Jake and Aunt Anna do it, too."

"Then keep it to yourself and don't tell anyone. Now go and make that bed."

Abraham and Ariel arrived the next afternoon. Ariel was a dark-haired, chunky version of Zach. He was soon chatting to the girls, and they found him great fun.

Abraham looked at Zach and said, "Isaac, my son, you look so well. You've grown, you look happy. Saul tells me I should be very proud of you and I am. Are you happy here, or do you want to come back?"

"I would like to stop here, please, Dad. I can be me here."

"Yes, son, I understand. Your college reports are so good, and Saul tells me you helped him solve a big case. Do you still want to follow him into the police?"

"Yes, I do. I've got an evening job now so I can pay you back some money. I have been saving it."

"No, son, I'll not take it. Give it to Saul or Anna for your keep. Your mother sends her love and I have a parcel for you. Rachel also sends her love and thanks you for the letters,"

"Has Granddad said anything?"

"Yes, that is the reason I am here. I need talk to Saul about him. He has finally agreed to meet Saul."

"Good, is it because I am here?"

"Partly and the trouble Malachi has caused, I need your input on that."

"What can I say? You know how I feel."

"Saul tells me you are almost a man grown and I should listen to you. He says you have a good brain and a wise head for your years. You can tell me things I wouldn't hear before."

"Oh, all right, father. You look thin and tired. Are you well?"

"Not very much. I have had a difficult time."

"I hope I was not the cause of this."

"No, boy, you were the revelation. Now, I must greet Anna."

"Yes, and did you know Jake and Aunty Di are coming? Let me take your bag to your room. Ariel is in with me."

The house filled up with Saul's family and five dogs and the evening became quite chaotic. Ariel went off with Stephen and Saul and the girls made a fuss of the two little boys, Little Saul and his brother Benjamin, while the older men talked.

Anna found Zach and said, "The others have gone down to the Green Dragon; don't you want to join them? I do."

Jake appeared and said, "Good idea, come on, Zach, let's get pissed; come on, Anna, you must join us."

They left and things quietened down. The girls were happily chatting with Nissa, the children's mother, and Abraham and Saul managed a long and rather serious conversation.

At about midnight, the party from the pub rolled in to find the house quiet. Nissa and the children had gone home, has had Tatum Sam's wife, and the girls had gone to bed. Abraham and Saul were playing chess in the lounge.

Saul looked up and groaned, "They're drunk, the lot of them. Here I am saying how sensible they are, and they roll in like this!"

Abraham laughed and said, "I can remember doing exactly the same Saul several times. I also remember our father being quite unreasonable about it; I hope we are not. They must learn how to hold their drink."

Saul stood up. "Stephen, Samuel your wives have gone home, I'll call a taxi for you."

"Thanks, Dad, a good idea. That was a brilliant evening."

"Ariel you are swaying, don't throw up here please, go to the cloakroom. Where is Zach?"

"Last seen trying to make it up the drive; Di was with him; she is helping Anna too."

"I will go and get them. Really, Abraham, we have a dreadful family!"

"Yes, I know. I'd forgotten how much fun it was. Just how much have you had, Ariel?"

"Too much. It was all Jake's fault."

"Yes, it always was. He, of course, has gone to sleep in that chair. Let's get you up to bed."

"You're not angry, Dad?"

"No, very amused. This brings back memories. I will be angry if Isaac throws up and makes a mess."

"All right, I'll try."

Saul turned to Di. "I thought you went to control things?"

"I did, then they threw down a challenge, I won. It is easy to tell they aren't drinkers, Abraham. Very lightweight. Poor Anna, she tried to keep up, Saul. I think you might need to get her up to bed. I'll help Zach,"

Jake, having woken up, said, "Thaks, Di, I love you; I'll try shime the clairs. My wobbles are all leggy. I'll ask the great tadpole in the sky to help."

Abraham began to laugh. "Get him to bed now. Tadpoles in the sky! I know just where that came from. They are going to feel dreadful tomorrow."

"Good, serves them right."

"When did you last get drunk, Abe?"

"It was with you and Jake years ago at our school reunion. I had to stay in your hotel room."

Saul had to stop Ariel and Zach singing about tadpoles about an hour later. He even had to get a bit cross with them and shut their door firmly on the way out. Grinning to himself, he looked in on Anna. "I knew it was a bad idea. Di is incredible. She is like a sponge. She is acting as sober as a judge. It's not fair; I'm going to have such a head in the morning."

"It's morning. I'm off today, I'll cope. You have a lie in. It is good to see you let your hair down."

"Being nice about it makes it worse. You'll never let me forget it!"

"I know, tough!"

Abraham, Saul, Di and the girls were the only ones to make it down for breakfast. Saul took them all out with the dogs to the park and they returned a couple of hours later to find Anna sluggishly moving around the kitchen.

Saul said, "Don't bother, we are going out for lunch. I rang The Star of David, and they can fit us in. Di, please rouse Jake and Abe, get your two up."

The restaurant was the best in town for kosha food. They went in a taxi minibus. It was a smart and expensive restaurant, and they were shown to a large circular table and ordered their food. Ariel helped the girls choose what they wanted. He explained what the food was.

The owner of the restaurant came over and said, "Saul, welcome. How wonderful to see you and you, Mr Catchpole. How is your son the rabbi? I found him very interesting when he spoke, but I didn't agree with a lot he said, but he spoke well."

"He is in London, still preaching. This is our brother, Jacob, and his wife, Diana. These are my other two sons, Ariel and Isaac, and my nieces, Sharon and Susan."

"Welcome all of you, and I hope you enjoy your meals."

Isaac looked at the food and said, "Great, I'm starving. Did I disgrace myself last night? If so, I am sorry."

"No, but you should have a massive hangover."

"I'm fine, but I think Ariel has one."

"Yes, I admit it. Why are you not angry with us?"

"Because, son, just occasionally, one needs to do it. Saul Jake and I did, Isaac, don't make a habit of it."

"No, Father."

The meal was a great success and that evening, when they were all in the lounge, Abraham said, "I need to ask for advice over Malachi from all of you. I need to know what has actually been going on. First, Isaac, I need you to tell me what went on at home when I was at work."

"He took over. Ordered us all around. He bullied Mother and took everything away from me and Rachel and locked them up so we couldn't use them. We were not allowed music, games or TV unless it was videos about the Holy Land, the Holocaust or Judaism. He would make us sit and listen to him reading scripture and then he would preach to us. When he was hungry, he would make Rachel or Mum go and get him food and I was sent to do any shopping they needed. He always timed me. He said it was your will, Dad, and you had asked him to."

"Yes, that is what Rachel and your mother say. Ariel, did he do this to you as well?"

"Yes, he did, or he tried until I went to work at the firm. He also locked Isaac in his room if he tried to protest. He didn't do it to me so much because I punched him when he tried once; I had got big enough. He told you I had punched him, and you punished me and wouldn't listen. He did not tell you the truth. Mother tried to but you wouldn't hear her either."

"For which I shall never forgive myself, I am so, so sorry. Ariel, you are a good son, hardworking and a joy to me. So, Isaac, are you! I will tell you what I have decided to do; as you know, after Isaac came up here, I asked Malachi to leave my house and I thought he had. He has his own flat. I have since been told that he has been coming back during the day and trying to spread his poison. My wife and Rachel are terrified of him. They tell me he is quite unhinged. Somehow, he still has a key."

"Change the locks, Abe."

"I have and the first time he met Rachel and took her key. The second time he took his mother's keys, he was waiting for her on the doorstep."

"He's violent?"

"Yes."

"So, what have you done?"

"I went to the senior rabbi and asked for his help. What he told me was a shock. Malachi was asked to leave some time ago; they saw he was far too extreme, and his behaviour was alarming them. He has joined a fanatical set in the East End, and it is thought that they are involved with several extreme groups. They warned me at the synagogue that he is refusing to listen to any of them and he is dangerous; he is no longer being paid; I have no idea where he gets his money. I do know that he has taken a lot from his mother. I also was told he had been over Germany last week."

"Doing what?"

"I don't know, Di. I rang him and asked to meet and when I did, I told him if he came to the house again, I would call the police. I asked him for his door key, and he denied having one; I asked him about Germany, and he threatened to get me committed because I was obviously ga ga; now what do I do? I admit I am frightened of him."

"Physically frightened?"

"Yes, Jake, I am. He threatened me, said I was senile and if I interfered with his work in any way, he would have committed and then send me to God. Where does he get this from?"

"You never knew father's elder brother, did you?"

"Uncle Joseph, the great Rabbi, No."

"I remember him. Horrid old man. I was only very small, just three, I think; I had heard children playing in the street outside; I didn't know if what they had said was swearing or blasphemy. I repeated what I had heard. He beat me so hard I still have the scars. He was vile, extreme and a zealot. That's where it comes from."

"Is that why you never swear?"

"I think so; it certainly put me off, Anna."

"Didn't you tell anyone?"

"No, if he came to the house, I hid. Then he died, and I said I was glad. Father beat me pretty hard for saying that, too. I never mentioned him again ever. I think I hated my father for that for a long time, for not knowing. Di, this extreme thing is more in your line."

"Yes, and I will chat with Ariel and Zach privately about it. I know about this group, The Millennium Reply. I must go and make some phone calls."

Zach said, "Yes, that's what he told us."

"Right, I will talk to you two later."

Di left the room.

Abraham looked at Zach and said, "How can I ever make it up to you?"

"I'm not sure you ever can. Let me stay here, please, if Uncle Saul and Aunt Anna will let me?"

Saul put his arm around Zach and said, "He has been a joy to both of us. He is far better behaved than my two lads were."

"Has he got into trouble?"

"Nothing to worry about, it is sorted."

Zach said, "I went too far when someone picked on me, Dad. Uncle Saul has rescued me."

"Like he did with us when we got into trouble as youngsters. I had better know what you did, though."

"I'll tell you before anyone else does. I smashed some glass in the greenhouse, fell into the pond, crashed a bike into a wall, scratched Aunt Anna's car and was told off for no lights on my bike, by Uncle Saul that was."

"Saul, I am so, so sorry all of these were bad."

"No, Abe, not nearly as bad as climbing up a drainpipe and bringing the whole lot down."

Jake began to laugh; Abe went red in the face and said, "Touché, I'd forgotten that."

Ariel, who had been listening with great interest, said, "What's this? Do tell."

"I'll tell you later, Ariel, Uncle Saul told me."

Jake grinned and said, "I was behind that; I egged him on. I always felt guilty about that. Sorry, Abe."

Saul said, "Good. I also remember the clock, the boat incident, the missing photos, the hiding of bacon in my room and many more. Boys will be boys; enough of this before you remember some things I did."

"That's just it. I can't. I do remember you being punished, but not what for."

"Then let us keep it like that, Jake. Now, the problem of Malachi. Change all the locks and use a keypad for a code and visitors can be recorded. If he keeps coming back, get an injunction. If you or Esther want to see him, go to him."

"I can't bring myself to disown him; he is my son."

Anna, who had been sitting listening to this with growing anger, said, "You were quick enough to disown the rest of the family, though, were you not? If he is the only one you care about, go and live with him and let the rest of the family live a normal, happy life. You need to sort out your priorities, Abe, and you need to do it now. I think this might be the last chance you are going to get with Isaac."

"And I am afraid with Rachel, Mum and me, Dad. If you love Malachi so much, go and be with him."

Abraham sat down very quickly on a chair and looked at everyone staring at him. It gradually dawned on him just how they felt. Then he thought back to the many times he had taken Malachi's side and how he had never considered anyone else or their feelings. The horror of what he had done overwhelmed him, and he burst into tears. Anna handed him a box of tissues and said, "Time to choose Abraham; whatever you decide now is what you will have to stick to."

"What have I done? My God, I have been foolish, wicked even. How can you ever forgive me? I see I cannot excuse it; I was so tied up in the respect and sticking to our faith I lost sight of what really mattered, and now I will tell you I want nothing more to do with Malachi."

"I suspect my wife will be dealing with him and his terrorist group, Abe. I also suggest you tell her whatever you know. Same for you, Ariel. You need to make up for what you allowed him to do with Zach."

"You're right Jake and I know it. Please forgive me Zach, tell me how I can put it right?"

"Dad, if anything has put me off our religion, it is you, Grandad, and Malachi. I will make my own decision about what if any, faith I follow. Yes, I forgive you, but it is the last time I do if you carry on putting Mal above any of the rest of us. None of us is perfect, I know that."

Saul looked at Isaac with a dawning respect. "Wise words Zach, it shows me you have maturity far beyond your years. I think we could all learn from this."

Saul moved over to the drinks cabinet as Di came back into the room. He poured and then handed Abraham a large whiskey. Leaving Di with Abraham, Ariel and Zach he took the rest of them out for a walk with the dogs. Diana had a long chat with Abraham and his two sons and when Saul came back in with the others, she said, "It is being dealt with. Say nothing to Malachi Abe; if you do, you will be suspected of being one of them."

Abe looked at her and said, "Thank you, Diana, you just pulled me back from the edge of a massive abyss. You have greatly eased my mind."

"It's my job; I am your sister-in-law, Abe."

"How can I repay or put right the wrongs I have done?"

"Well, to start with, I know Saul needs a new suit. He seems fated to wreck one every six months. Now, who's hungry?"

About a week later, Saul came into the general squad office after lunch to find most of the squad huddled around a screen and laughing heartily. He crept up behind them to see what was causing such amusement.

Tarik turned and saw him, cleared his throat and said, "Guys, we have the star of the show here."

Saul said, "I had better see what you all find so amusing then."

The clip was replayed, and Saul realised that someone had filmed the time when he and Zach had gone into the lake in the park to get the dogs out and stop them from attacking the fountains.

When he watched it, he could not help but laugh as it was very funny. "OK, who is the guilty party then?"

Simon, one of the detectives, said, "A mate of mine saw it, sir, and thought I would like to. It's wonderful."

"Yes, maybe, now. Round everyone up for the briefing."

When everyone was assembled, Saul told them how the cases were progressing and when they would be required to give evidence.

He then said, "Alan Withers is off on leave at the moment as Caroline has started labour. He promises to tell me as soon as the child is born. Geoff, I think you can organise all the usual welfare gifts and cards. That is the good news; I know several of you have been visiting Fred Dunlop and he and his wife were very appreciative. I am sad to say but Fred died this morning. I will expect a full turnout at the funeral, which I will inform you of when I know the details. Des Trotter has come back on full duties and during his sick leave, he took the opportunity to study and has passed his promotion exams. As have you, Simon. Well, done! I have here a letter that was sent to the chief constable and he has asked me to read it to you; it is from the firm Atkins and Atkins, the auctioneers."

"Dear Chief Constable. I would like to formally express thanks and gratitude for the work of your officers, who were so thorough and industrious over the incidents when Herbert Yorke and Eric Ross were killed at our premises. Not only have the murders been successfully detected, but your officers have also detected a huge fraud against this company. Had they not done so, I fear we would have had to go out of business. To this end, we have consulted with the Police Authority and have offered a yearly scholarship for any officer from this area who is in need of some support. This will be accompanied by an annual award to an officer who has excelled in their duties. Again, may I offer our profound thanks, William Atkins Senior and William Atkins Junior."

There was a round of applause and Saul held up his hand and said, "I would also like to add my thanks to you for all the hard work and dedication you have shown through this enquiry. The chief has accepted, and the award will be called the Fred Dunlop Award. I managed to tell Fred a couple of days ago and he was so happy. Now, as you know, when there is not a current murderer enquiry, anyone who has left to take and wants to take it may do so. I, too, have to take some leave for personal reasons, so until my return, you will be managed by Inspector Bickerstaff, who will be acting up. I will be in my office for the next hour or so if anyone needs to see me. Simon, please would you be kind enough to let me have a copy of that video? My family would love it, especially my nephew."

When Saul got home later that afternoon, he sat down at the kitchen table with Anna and Zack. "Since Abraham went back to London, things have been developing. I thought you were very forgiving, Zach, and I trust your father sees how much you have grown up and what a fine young man you are. He rang yesterday and told me several things have changed; my father wishes to see me and has asked me to go down to London to see him; he has also extended the invitation to you, Zach, if you want to come. He then said he could hardly blame you if you didn't, if you never wanted to see him again. Anna has agreed to stay here with the girls, but I ask you to consider his request, and if you do want to come, I am leaving first thing in the morning."

"I'm not sure. Can I have a little time to think on it?"

"Before I go, I need to bring you up to date. The group that Malachi belonged to were all arrested this morning, both here and in other countries. Malachi is amongst them."

"What will happen to him?"

"He can preach to the walls of his cell; he's going to prison almost certainly. He has been watched very closely for long enough to prove he is one of the ringleaders."

"Yes, Diana has been away a lot recently, hasn't she?"

"You're so quick you'll cut yourself. Why did you not tell what you knew about him before?"

"That's easy, I tried. Not even my own family would listen to me, when I came here, I thought you wouldn't either. Tell me Uncle Saul, when your uncle beat you for swearing why did you not tell anyone?"

"For the same reason, I suppose. Point taken. What I do know is that your father is in a very dark place because of what Malachi has done. He is racked with guilt over the way he treated you and the others in the family. The hardest thing for him to do was tell your grandfather. Their world has fallen apart. I am hoping I might be able to put things in perspective, but it will be a bit like sticking a plaster on a severed artery."

"If I do come with you, I want to know I can come back here. I do not want to stay there or feel morally obligated to. This house is now my home."

"Yes, and it always will be Zach. Saul and I agreed on that. We talked it over last night while you were out working. Not only do we think you are happier here, but we are also happier too. If necessary and if it will help, we are quite happy to become your legal guardians. I am afraid I am not as forgiving as either of you; I think the sooner you are away from London, the happier it will make you. Yes, I think you should go and sort things out but come back to us, please?"

"Aunt Anna, thank you. Yes, I will go, if only for my mother's sake."

The trip to London was harrowing for both of them; Saul spoke at length with his father and Isaac with his parents and sister and Ariel. They stayed three nights and then drove back. On the journey, Zach got progressively more cheerful the further they got from London.

Zach was talking about his course at college and then said, "Oh, and I did some research and found some interesting things out about the auction mart. Did you know it is built on the site of a very old mansion?"

"No."

"It's very odd. The place was burned down twice, and there was some sort of battle there when Skipton Castle was under siege. I looked further in the records and found there was a massive betrayal there and several murders. The whole area is steeped in history, most of it rather unpleasant. Mysterious things have always happened there. While I was at the library, I ran into old Mr Atkins. I like him. He asked me what I was doing. I told him about the history of the mart. He said he knew some of the history but then asked if I knew the mart was haunted. He said he had never seen anything, but others had. He also mentioned a huge murder case last year near there."

"Yes, I dealt with that nasty business. I am still waiting to give evidence at court on that."

"Well, all this nastiness got me thinking, too, so I started looking at the para-psychic sites. I got some good books out, too. The ghost stories are well documented. Don't tell Dad, please; he thinks all that is nonsense. In fact, he would never let us read any spooky stories at all."

"No, he wouldn't. Have you ever read a book called Ghost Stories of an Antiquary by MR James?"

"No."

"I'll lend it to you. Don't read it at bedtime!"

"Thanks. You wondered why all those cases sort of collided with each other at the mart. I've a theory. Could the place be a catalyst for evil, or hatred that sort of haunts the place?"

"It is possible, I suppose but I doubt it. Now tell me how did you get on with your father?"

"He was great. He gave me the most profound apology and begged my forgiveness. He said he want nothing more to do with Mal and if I want to go back, I will always be welcome, but he also thinks I will do very well with you. Not once did he talk about religion. He has changed I think."

"So, what have you decided?"

"I told him I had forgiven him, but I could not forget, so I would be making my home with you, and he accepted that. He also said he hoped I would be a good police officer and follow you. How did you get on with Grandad? Who was also very nice to me."

"Better than I had hoped. We talked a lot. Abe had told him everything, even about my uncle beating me. He asked me about it, so I told him. It actually hurt a lot doing that. He said it was a small wonder I had been put off our religion and he apologised. When he found out what Malachi had done to you, especially to your father, he said he wished he had died and didn't have to live with the shame of it. He said he wanted to keep in touch. I gave him pictures of all the family, including you, and he accepted them."

"Do you forgive him?"

"I suppose so. I think I did years ago. He is the product of his generation and his strict religious upbringing. Since my mother died, he no longer lives in the real world; he has his room, his wireless and his faith. Outside, he is a stranger in a strange world. His stroke means he can't really get out and I don't think he wants to."

"That's sad!"

"Yes, very, but he is content with what he knows. He was in the army, you know. He volunteered and lied about his age to get in. A lot of Jewish boys did. And fought and died bravely. He was in the Army of Occupation and went to Auschwitz. What he saw and learned there did something horrible to him. His mind and soul. My mother told me he would never speak about what he saw."

"I didn't know any of that, does Dad?"

"I don't think so. He gave his medals to give to you and Ariel when he died. When he was talking about what Malachi had done, he broke down and cried. I think I got closer to him in the last three days than I have ever been."

"Did he ask about Jake?"

"Yes, he did, and he says he forgives him and hopes he does well. He gave me letters to several people. I think he is putting his house in order."

"He thinks he is going to die soon?"

"Yes, somehow, he knows the time is soon. He says he is looking forward to it so he can be with my mother again. He adored her. He is very grateful to your mother, too."

"Are you very sad, Uncle Saul?"

"Yes, in a way, but also relieved, I've finally put things right. Thanks for being there for me Zach, I appreciate it."

Saul's father died a month later. The funeral was conducted as he had requested, with all his offspring there, except Malachi, who was in a high-security prison. The family returned to Abraham's house and when all the funeral guests had gone, Saul took Abraham aside and said, "Abe, I have a last request from father that I must carry out. I need you with me. Can we go?"

In the car, Saul explained, and they arrived at the high-security prison where they were seen by the duty governor who said, "Yes, you explained on the phone, and yes, he will see you. What is this gift you have for him?"

"It is here, a Pentateuch, my father's copy of The Holy Scripture and a carved Star of David, carved in bone. Please examine them, as I know you have to. They are delicate and precious but not dangerous. They will mean something special to Malachi. How did he take the news of his grandfather's death?"

"Rather badly. He demanded go to the service but that was out of the question."

"Nor would he have been welcome there; I have a letter from my father to give him. It was written after Malachi's arrest. Here, you will want to read it, I expect."

The governor read the letter and handed it back to Saul. After the normal security checks, they were shown into a room and Malachi was brought in.

The warden said, "Any problems, just press the button. We will be monitoring from just outside."

Malachi looked thin and drawn. He said, "Father, forgive me. I have been a total fool. How could I be so stupid and arrogant? I have had time to think in here."

"Time much needed Malachi. I will not cast you off as my father did to Saul and Jake, but I cannot defend what you have done or the way you treated us. If Isaac can forgive you and Rachel, then I will try. The scriptures teach us forgive. I will try but it is going to be very hard."

Malachi turned to Saul. "Uncle Saul, can you forgive me?"

"I don't know. You have done great harm and must now face the consequences. I had a long talk with your grandfather before he died; he asked me to write this at his dictation and give it to you on his death."

Malachi read the letter, "Yes, I see. There is much wisdom in it and many things to study. No wonder he did not want me there today. I must accept and learn from it. I shall keep this to remind me."

"It is between you and him. I was merely the scribe. He also asked me to dispose of some of his things. I thought these might give you some solace. He brought all these back from Auschwitz, where he was just after the war."

Saul handed over the five scrolls in their covers and the bone star. He then gave him the Book of Scripture. Malachi asked, "I do not understand why you are being so kind after the way I treated you and your family."

"Because I love all my family. Maybe you will learn from what he said, and it will remind you of where hatred can lead. I see the results of hatred too often and know how dreadful it can be. I have quite recently seen what looked like a loving family, but it was where all but the father and the son were cruelly treated, despised and abused. The father and the son thought they were the only ones who mattered. As soon as you put yourself in such an arrogant category, you show just how evil a man can be. You now have the opportunity of putting right a lot of what you have done. I trust you will take it. All life is sacred and it is not for you to judge. Judge not and ye shall not be judged. Our god is a forgiving god. Only he will judge fairly."

"Yes, my grandfather said."

"I know what he said. That is now between you and your conscience; I've had my say, Malachi. I will now leave you to talk to your father."

Saul left the room and was taken to a seating area by the governor. "Wise words, Mr Catchpole. I hope he heeds them. I hope it is not an act. He has had long sessions with our rabbi."

"We will have to wait and see if I can help; I will; I have a few contacts in the legal world."

"Oh, I know who you are."

"You do?"

"Yes, we have several lifers in here that you put here. Your name comes up quite often."

"I expect it does; they must hate my guts."

"Not really. Some do, but accept you had a job to do, some even admire you. We do try to rehabilitate you know."

When Abraham got in the car outside the prison, Saul looked at him. "Can I say anything to comfort you, little brother?"

"I doubt it. That was the hardest thing I have ever done. What did father say in that letter? It seemed to affect him."

"If Malachi wants you to know, he will show you. I was just the scribe. Now, I had better get you home and take my lot back to Yorkshire."

"Thank you so much, Saul, for all you have done."

"It's my job, little brother. I'm head of the family now. I have a duty to be pompous, overbearing, dictatorial, inflexible, bossy, and strict!"

"And Jake and I, as your younger brothers have a duty; it's our job to cut you down to size, burst your bubble of pomposity and generally argue with you."

"That's all right then. Of course you do; I'd be seriously worried if you didn't."

The End.